BONE
MUSIC

David Almond

HODDER

HODDER CHILDREN'S BOOKS
First published in Great Britain in 2021 by Hodder and Stoughton

This paperback edition published in 2021

1 3 5 7 9 10 8 6 4 2

A CIP catalogue record for this book is available from the British Library.

ISBN 978 1 444 95292 6

Typeset in Bembo by Avon DataSet Ltd, Arden Court, Alcester, Warwickshire

Printed and bound in Great Britain by
Clays Ltd, Elcograf S.p.A.

The paper and board used in this book
are made from wood from responsible sources.

Hodder Children's Books
An imprint of Hachette Children's Group
Part of Hodder and Stoughton
Carmelite House
50 Victoria Embankment
London EC4Y 0DZ

An Hachette UK Company
www.hachette.co.uk

www.hachettechildrens.co.uk

BONE MUSIC

Also by David Almond

Skellig

My Name is Mina

Kit's Wilderness

Heaven Eyes

Counting Stars

Secret Heart

The Fire Eaters

Clay

Jackdaw Summer

Wild Girl, Wild Boy – A Play

Skellig – A Play

A Song for Ella Grey

The Colour of the Sun

For Freya

She felt like a ghost. She woke in the night. What was that music? Some troubled beast? Some strange bird of the night? Some lost soul wandering on the moors? Just her dreams?

What wild and weird things existed here?

Sylvia got up from her narrow bed, went to the window, held open her thin curtains, dared to peep.

Nothing. Darkness everywhere.

Darkened street below, darkness of the undulating land, blackness of the forest at the village's edge, light of a farmhouse far, far off, pale glow on the southern horizon, immensity of stars above.

The noise softened, became more lyrical. Whistle-like, flute-like, bird-like. Her head reeled as the music came into her. She narrowed her eyes and tried to see.

Nothing.

It was like something she'd dreamed before, like something coming from inside her as well as from outside her, like something she'd heard before. But how could she have? She couldn't have.

Stop being stupid, Sylvia, she whispered to herself. *Stop being so weird.*

She widened her eyes again, looked at the stars, the galaxies, the great spirals and clusters of light. The universe, spinning and dancing through time. Why was it all so huge? Why was she so small?

What the hell was she doing out here in this empty ancient place?

The music faltered, became jagged again, a series of groans and squeaks, as if it couldn't maintain the sweetness in itself. Was that a dark swaying human shape, there against the darkness of the forest's edge? Was it moving back into the forest? Or was it just her dreams, continuing?

The music ended, left its weird rhythms in her. Some tiny star-thing drifted gently through the black and glittering heavens.

Why had her bliddy mother brought her here? What weird stuff went on out here? What weird things existed here?

No answers.

She left the window, went back to her bed.

Checked her phone. No signal.

She yearned for the city again, she yearned for a signal.

Stop it, Sylvia, she told herself. *Calm down. It's only for a bliddy week or two.*

She closed her eyes.

The dancing in her mind faltered and slowed.

She slept.

'Good morning, my lovely! Sleep well, my love?'

Next morning. Her mum, in the little kitchen, pouring muesli into bowls. Yoghurt and a bowl of berries on the table, a pot of coffee. She stirred the coffee then poured, then made a swirl of white milk on top. Steam and the delicious scent rose.

'Ah, it's sulky Sylvia today, is it?' she said.

She came to Sylvia and put her arms around her.

Sylvia shrugged. 'Aye,' she muttered.

She pushed the grains and berries round and round her bowl.

On the floor were the boxes of food they'd brought with them, a case of red wine. And her mum's sketchbooks and pencils and paints and brushes and knives and palettes and canvases. A couple of easels against the wall. A half-finished painting of a desert scene. A scattering of photographs.

'Hear anything?' Sylvia said.

'Anything?'

'In the night. Like music or something.'

'Nope. Slept like a babe, thank goodness.'

'Like a babe?'

'Maybe it's the darkness, maybe it's the silence.'

'Any news of Dad?'

'Nope. He'll be fine. He always liked a bit of silence, didn't he? He's probably drinking in some five-star hotel with his mates. Hold still a minute, will you?'

'What? *Mum*!'

Mum had a pencil and sketchbook in her hands. She was sketching, drawing.

'Chin up a bit,' she said.

'No!'

'I've got to get back into it, haven't I? Turn to the left a bit, eh?'

Sylvia scowled.

'Yes, that's a good expression,' said her mum. 'Hold that a moment.'

'*Mum!*'

'Oh Sylvia, calm down. If there's news, it'll get to us. It's not like we're in Outer Mongolia, is it?'

'Might as well be.'

'We're not even fifty miles from Newcastle! Anyway, what kind of music?'

Sylvia shrugged. 'Dunno. Probably nowt. Must have been dreaming.'

She looked through the window. Pale houses across the narrow roadway, sunlight, the forest's edge, a far dark hillside. A black bird, flapping past, then another, then another. Other birds, dozens of them, much higher up, swirling and spiralling. And sky, sky, bliddy endless sky.

'There's lots of music out this way,' her mother said. 'Pipers, fiddlers. Mebbe there was a dance going on somewhere.'

Sylvia sighed.

A dance? What kind of dance took place out here?

'Think I'll . . .' she started.

5

'Think you'll what?'

Sylvia scowled again. Aye, exactly. What *did* she think she'd do out here? Set off walking back to the town? She stood up and got her coat from the back of the door. Got her scarf. Held her hands out wide. Her mum went on sketching.

'I'll do what there is to do here, Mum. I'll open the door, go out into the emptiness and then I'll turn round and come back in again.'

'That's a good idea, love. You have a nice walk. You should put your boots on.'

The boots? No way. She pulled her pale blue canvas shoes on.

Mum put her arms around Sylvia again. Sylvia let her do so.

'It'll do us good,' said her mum. 'A few days away in a beautiful place. And God, to get away from those kids for a while!'

'You love those kids.'

'Aye, but I need a holiday from all of it!'

Sylvia clenched her fists and stood dead still.

'Sorry,' she said. 'I know you need it, Mum.'

'Thanks, love. Now go on, off you go.'

Sylvia pulled the door open.

There was a chill breeze. There was sky, going on forever.

She sighed and stepped out.

'Don't get lost,' her mum said gently.

She put her hand to Sylvia's back and guided her away.

This was it, the village. Two rows of narrow timber houses, most of them faded white, some of them painted in would-be jolly shades: yellow, orange, an incredibly ugly purple one. Each had a patch of garden, a low wicket fence. Some flowers dancing in the breeze. A few cars, a couple of pick-ups, a couple of white transit vans. A long-abandoned telephone box. A long, low timber shack with BLACKWOOD COMMUNITY CLUB painted on it. A fading poster with a crude picture of a fiddle and some pipes. Another poster headed:

REWILDING THE NORTH
Should the Lynx Come Back?

There was an artist's impression of a lynx on a forest

path, its ears pointed, its fur spotted, its head turned to look out at the observer.

She grinned at the graffiti that was scribbled across it: **YES! And Lions and Tigers and Bears as well.**

'And wildebeest,' she muttered. 'And elephants and anteaters and kangaroos.'

She walked on along the single potholed roadway.

Came to a grey timber chapel with slipped slates, boards on its windows and padlocks on its doors. There was an ancient crucifix on the gable end. A battered Jesus dangled from a single nail through his hand. He swayed awkwardly in the breeze. A message was painted on the wall below.

He Died So That We Might Live

At one end of the village, the roadway narrowed, turned into a track that led towards the dark forest. At the other end, it led to yawning light-filled spaces. She turned around and headed for the light. A few folk about. A frail-looking pale and ancient man in a white flat-cap sat in a deckchair outside his front door. He raised a hand in greeting.

She nodded back at him.

'You will be the Allens, I would say,' he said.

His voice was accented, not from this place. European.

'The Allens?' she said.

'Yes, I think so.'

And yes, of course, it was true. That was her mother's maiden name.

'Aye,' she said. 'We are, I suppose.'

He lifted a striped mug of something from the little table beside him and swigged.

There was a row of stones arranged neatly on his window frame.

'I am Andreas Muller,' he said. His eyes were kind and watery. 'Welcome back to you.'

She didn't linger. She didn't want to talk. She didn't think to tell him what her name was.

She walked on. There was a little swings park on a fenced-off cindery patch behind the houses. A boy or a girl was there, and an ancient rusty swing squeak-squeak-squeaked as they swung on it.

She thought of Maxine. She said she'd call. She looked at her phone. No signal. Of course no bliddy signal.

Some high birds whirled and screeched.

She walked on. The roadway veered away through the empty turf and bracken across the moors. No traffic on it. At the village's edge a footpath sign pointed north into the emptiness. It bore a cartoon of a jolly walker striding on. She stopped. This was the furthest north she'd been, the furthest-flung she'd ever been. Heather, bracken, yellow gorse, a million scattered sheep. Stone walls, streams. A handful of ruined cottages that must once have been part of the village. A derelict farmhouse with herd of hardly-moving stocky cattle by it. The moors, the fells, or whatever the damn things were called, and black rocks and jagged crags, and all of them mounting higher, turning to dark lumps and bulges on the impossibly far horizon.

And over everything the empty massive sky.

And back beyond the village, the dark and endless-looking forest.

This is where her mum had been a baby. They'd told Sylvia about the place when she was a tot. She'd seen the photographs, she'd seen the paintings. She'd known exactly what it would be like. They hadn't brought her then. She was a city girl. Why bring her here now?

She closed her eyes against it all. She kept back tears.

Don't be stupid, Sylvia, she told herself. *You'll soon be back at home.*

'Will you be my sister?'

She flinched, she turned.

A boy, in jeans and a white shirt, long flaxen hair. She looked past him, saw the swing swinging empty now.

'Will you?' he said. 'I haven't got one yet.'

'I don't even know you.'

What was she doing even answering him?

'That doesn't matter,' he said. 'I wouldn't know a sister if she'd just been born, would I? And she wouldn't know me.'

'Go away.'

He didn't move.

'No,' she said. 'I won't be. Go away. Go away.'

He laughed.

His eyes were big, blue, shining.

'I've got a brother,' he said, 'so he could be yours and all.'

'I don't want a brother. I don't want you. Why would I?'

'He's called Gabriel,' he said. 'It would be like in the olden days.'

The olden days? What the hell was he on about?

'When all the children were here,' he said.

She turned away, took the track of the cartoon striding man.

'My name's Colin!' he called after her.

She walked on.

'I know you're Sylvia Carr!' he called.

'Thanks for letting me know,' she whispered.

She didn't turn. She walked. The path climbed gently. She headed higher, seeking a signal. She tugged her collar up against her throat. The breezes swirled around her, blew her hair about her head. The ground was soft, moist. Sometimes dark water seeped around her feet. Something scuttled in the grass. A single hawk hovered above a crag.

And far far off, a black jet flew fast and low above the horizon. So beautiful, so elegant, so swift, so silent, as if it couldn't hurt a fly.

Her dad used to laugh and call her mum a child of the forest. A wild child. He said she was a fellow of the deer and the fox.

'Or even of the bear,' he said. 'Weren't there bears

up there when you were a bairn?'

'Yes!' her mum would say. 'And wolves and antelopes as well.'

For a while, as an infant, Sylvia had believed all this. She'd giggle and grin when he held her chin in his hand and looked deep into her eyes.

'You're another one,' he said. 'Feral kid of a feral mum. There's a bit of fox in you, I think, a dose of the eagle. Looks like I'm the only civilised one among us.'

In truth, her mum had spent just the first months of her life here. The village had been built for the forest workers, which was what her mum's dad, her grandfather, had been. They planted the forest, helped it to grow, harvested it. It became one of the great forests of the north. But times changed. There were more machines. Fewer humans were needed. Her family, and lots of other families, moved away to find new work, new lives. Her grandfather opened the little sweet shop on Heaton Road. He never went back again.

And her mother had never gone back either. Till now, when she'd come to do some art, to get away, to bring her daughter with her.

Sylvia pulled her collar close. No signal. Maxine would be with Francesca today. They'd be going to jazz at Live tonight. Mickey was doing drums. His first proper gig.

There were scuttlings and scratchings all around her. The wind cried in the grass. She should have worn the walking boots her mum had bought for her and made her bring. The seeping water had soaked and darkened her pale canvas shoes. Her feet were wet. Water everywhere. It glistened in little pools on the path, it trickled, it sparkled in streams that ran down the hillsides. And as she got higher, she saw the flat dark surface of Kielder Water in the distance. Its dark dense forest rose from its banks.

Footsteps behind her.

That kid again. Colin. He was panting. He'd been walking fast.

'Got to show you something,' he said.

She groaned.

'You want to see?' he said.

He reached down and tugged at a blade of grass. Tore off a short piece of it. Put it between his thumbs, lifted his thumbs to his lips and blew.

A squeak. Of course there was a squeak. All kids

did it. She'd done it in the garden with Maxine when she was a little girl.

'Hear?' he said.

She said nothing.

'You want a go?'

She said nothing.

'My brother showed me how to do it.'

Just go away, she wanted to say.

'Listen again,' he said.

He blew again. He tilted his head back and made a longer, louder, more undulating note. He stopped and held his arms out in the empty air.

'Listen,' he said. 'Hear it?'

'Hear what?'

'It makes them sing.'

'Makes what sing?'

'The birds. When I do it, the birds sing back. Listen, that's a curlew.'

'They were singing anyway.'

'Some of them were. But not that one. Hear it? It heard me and it's calling back to me. That's what music does out here.'

She sighed.

'OK,' she said.

'My brother does it. He can get anything singing. He can call foxes out, and badgers, and deer. How old are you?'

'What?'

'You must be fifteen or something. That's what he is too. I'm only nine. I go to school in Hexham. He doesn't go to school.'

'Why aren't you at school today?'

'Bad belly. Anyway, school just makes you stupid, doesn't it?'

'Does it?'

'Yes. Fills you up with rotten rubbish. Bet you go to school, don't you?'

'Yes.'

'Poor you.'

He blew the grass again.

'That's what you should learn in school,' he said.

She groaned. Kids, what were they like?

'He says if you get really good at it,' he said, 'you can call any animal you want to call and it'll come to you.'

She rolled her eyes.

'With a blade of grass?' she said.

'No, not just with grass. With other things.'

He blew again.

The birds sang and the wind cried.

And far away, another swift and silent jet streaked above the fells.

'He says,' he said, 'that if you get really *really* good at it, you can see ghosts in the forest and call bodies out of the ground.'

She shook her head. Why was she standing here talking to him?

'Go away, Colin,' she groaned.

'Where's he this time?'

'Where's who?'

'Your dad. He's always off somewhere, taking pictures, isn't he?'

'What's it got to do with you? He's nowhere.'

'He's got to be somewhere. Stands to reason, doesn't it?'

She said nothing, just stared back at him.

'Do you think he might get killed?' he asked.

She shook her head, she closed her eyes.

'I don't think he will,' he said.

When she looked again, he was walking back down the hill towards the village. His pale hair shone in the sun, and he swung his arms as if dancing or flying.

She watched him go.

She shook her head at the thought of having him as a brother. She'd never wanted such a thing. A sister, maybe. That'd be different. She didn't miss such a thing, she'd always been a happy child, but she'd toyed with the notion as a little girl. She'd even imagined a girl turning up one day just as Colin had, and taking her hand and asking, Can I be your sister? And the two of them walking through Heaton Park together, hand in hand.

She laughed at the memory. Kids. What it was to be a child.

She walked on. She went higher.

No signal. She cursed the air. What was a signal, anyway? When there was a signal and she heard Maxine's voice, how did the voice get into the phone? Was the voice somehow in the air around her? Was it like the birdsong, like the wind? How did it squeeze into something like a phone? Was it only a phone that could catch such things? Mickey said once that a phone was like a wand. You held it in the air and it drew voices to it. You used it to wave messages away from it. Magic. Could her ear be a wand? Could her head?

She closed her eyes and tilted her head and listened.

Maxine, she whispered. *I'm calling to you. Maxine, I'm listening for you.*

She cursed again. *A week out here and I'll be bliddy mental*, she thought.

But she listened again. She whispered into the air again. She looked at the air and realised you couldn't look at the air. It was just space and nothingness. But it wasn't empty. You couldn't see, but it was full of stuff. Wind and light and noises and messages and . . .

You will, Sylvia, she said. *You'll turn bliddy barmy.*

She stood dead still with her arms held high above her head with her fingers reaching into the empty air – a mast, a receiver, a wand.

'Let me receive you!' she said.

'Speak to me,' she whispered.

'Come to me,' she sighed. 'Please come to me.'

The air seemed to shudder a moment. There came a muffled boom, like a distant explosion. Then another. Then silence. She scanned the horizons. Nothing to see.

She abandoned the search for a signal.

She listened to the birdsong, to the breeze in the grass.

She breathed in deeply, breathed out.

Smiled.

'Now, Sylvia,' she said to herself in the tone of voice that Maxine would use, 'calm down. Just try thinking of it all in a different way.'

'OK,' she said to herself and to Maxine. 'I will do that.'

She looked around.

She relaxed. She had to admit that yes, it really was beautiful.

She took a blade of grass.

Put it between her thumbs and blew.

A curlew cried.

She blew again.

Another cry.

'Thank you, curlew,' she said.

She breathed in the air, gazed at the beauty, then went down the hill again.

Her mother was with Andreas Muller, sitting on his bench with him before his little table.

'Come and see, Sylvia!' she called.

Sylvia went through the little gate. There was a

pot of tea, a jug of milk and some mugs on the table. And there were some of the stones from the window ledge. She saw that they weren't ordinary stones. They were blades and axes, ancient tools. She'd seen pictures of things like this before, but she'd never seen the real thing.

'This is Herr Muller, Sylvia,' her mum said. 'Herr Muller, this is Sylvia.'

'We have already met,' he said.

He held his hand out. Sylvia took it.

'Hello,' she said.

'I've told him all about you,' said her mum.

'Maybe not *all*,' said Andreas.

They all smiled. Andreas blushed, as she did.

'Andreas *remembers* me!' said her mum.

'Remembers you?'

'He was here when I was born. He was here when I left.'

'She was a baby,' he said. 'A bonny bairn, as babies are. But not much to remember, really. You appeared, and you quickly went away.'

'And Andreas has been here all this time, Sylvia.'

She laughed.

'It seems *impossible*!' she said.

21

Andreas smiled. He seemed so frail. He took a deep breath and it rattled softly in his throat.

'And long before that too,' he said. 'This beautiful place has been my home, my refuge, for a long time. Would you like some tea?'

She sat on a stool formed from a sawn-off tree trunk by the table.

Andreas poured her tea into a mug with an image of soaring swifts on it.

She drank. It was delicious.

He lifted one of the stones and let it rest on his trembling hand. A flat black stone with a curved edge, nearly as big as his palm.

'It is flint,' he said. 'A scraping tool. Take it, Sylvia.'

She took it from him.

'It is for scraping the flesh from skin, we believe, for the making of leather or fur. Take care with the edge. It is sharp.'

She gazed down at it.

'It is perhaps five thousand years old,' he said. 'Perhaps older.'

It rested gently on her skin. She saw the carefully shaped edge.

'I should like to give it to you,' Andreas said.

'To me?' she said.

'Yes. A little token of welcome.'

It was so beautiful, so balanced, so well made. She tried to imagine scraping an animal skin with it, and could not. What would the skin feel like? Would there be blood? And the smell?

'Are you sure?' she said.

'Yes. Though of course, it is not truly mine to give. I pass it on, as you will pass it on. A little message from the dim and distant past. And a message to the future.'

She didn't know what to say.

'Thank you,' she said. 'I'll look after it.'

'Maybe it was used by someone just like you, Sylvia.'

Like me? she thought. Could that really be true?

'These things lie waiting to be found, just below the surface,' he said. 'There are many of them. Farmers expose them when they plough their fields. Rabbits kick them out when they dig their burrows. I uncover them when I scrape at the earth with my trowel.'

Sylvia touched the stones.

'The past is all around us,' said Andreas. 'It is just beneath us. It is deep within us.'

Sylvia tried to imagine the people who had made

them, used them, and she could not.

'They were just like us,' Andreas said. 'The people of the past.'

'Were they?'

'The same bodies,' he said, 'the same minds. The baby that your mother was could have been a baby from six thousand years ago. The girl that you are now could have been a girl six thousand years ago. Dressed differently, of course, with a name that is not Sylvia, and of course the surroundings would be rather different – but you? Same body. Same mind. Same human being.'

Again she wondered, *Could it be true?*

'Perhaps,' Andreas said, 'the ancient Sylvia is just below the surface of the modern you.'

She lifted another of the stones, a longer, narrower brown-coloured gleaming thing with a point at its end. She tried to imagine that her hands were the hands of an ancient Sylvia as she held it and felt it.

'Be care—' said Andreas.

Too late. She touched the point with the tip of her index finger. Razor sharp. A sudden sting. It drew blood immediately. A tiny incision into her skin and flesh.

'Oh, Sylvia!' gasped her mum.

She took Sylvia's hand and lifted it to her lips as if to lick, as she would have when Sylvia was small.

Sylvia laughed at that. She licked the bulbs of blood away herself. It'd soon stop. She wondered what else this knife had cut in its long life.

'The perfect blade,' Andreas said. 'To be still so sharp after so many years.'

He wiped Sylvia's blood from the blade with a tissue.

'Just like us,' he said, 'they made tools to create and tools to kill. You could take this too, if you'd like to.'

He handed it back to her.

'Are you sure?' said her mum.

'If that is OK with you,' said Andreas. 'I have found many of them. They are not so rare. And she knows now how careful she must be with it.'

Sylvia held it carefully.

'It's beautiful,' she said.

'It is. And here is something to keep it in and keep you safe.'

He gave her a soft brown leather pouch. She folded it around the blade.

'Sylvia has been worried,' said her mum, 'by coming

to the silence and darkness out here.'

Andreas laughed. 'Yes, it can be very . . . disconcerting. You will get used to it.'

Sylvia shrugged.

'And in truth,' said Andreas, 'there is really no such thing as silence. And where is there darkness without any light?'

She said nothing.

The adults started talking of the days when the village was inhabited by foresters and their families. She let them ramble on. She brushed away the dried flakes of blood from her skin. She gazed over the rooftops and the forest into the empty sky and tried again to imagine being a girl from five thousand years ago. Would her body really have been the same? Would her mind? Could it be true? She was Sylvia Carr, a girl of the twenty-first century, a girl troubled by wars, by disgraceful politicians, by global heating, a girl who yearned for hope, for things to change. Could she also be an ancient Sylvia Carr?

She took the knife from its pouch again. If there was a way to look closely enough at it, would she be able to see the traces of another's blood on it, from thousands of years ago? If she felt deeply enough, would she be able to feel the touch of other hands from long, long ago?

She heard Andreas mention war.

'War?' she said.

'Yes,' said Andreas. 'I came here as a prisoner of war.'

He smiled at her confusion.

'A war that must seem so very long ago to you,' he said. 'I was captured in France and I was brought here.'

'World War two?'

'Yes. They put me into a prisoner of war camp nearby. When peace came, they sent me home. But I knew I had to come back. This would be my true home.'

'How *old* are you?' said Sylvia.

'Sylvia!' her mum said.

'That's OK,' he said. 'I am ancient. I'm ninety-five years old, Sylvia.'

He laughed.

'Maybe I should be a ghost by now.'

Sylvia began to imagine him as a ghost.

'Just think,' he said, 'when I was your age, Sylvia, I would have been your enemy.'

She swigged her cooling tea.

'It would have been our duty,' he said, 'to destroy each other.'

They all pondered that.

'To destroy each other,' Andreas went on, 'and then to reconstruct each other.'

He laughed and poured more tea.

'How crazy we are, we humans.'

That evening, she got her walking boots from the car and put them in the little hallway. She hung her waterproof jacket on a hook on the back of the front door. She unpacked her suitcase and hung up her clothes in the narrow wardrobe in her room. She laid out her toiletries in the tiny bathroom. She put a sketchbook and pencils by the bed. She put her book on the pillow. She sat with her mum at the dining table. They ate lasagne and salad. Her mum drank white wine.

There was no TV, no Wi-Fi, no landline.

Her mum put some ancient pyjamas on. She sighed as she talked about the peace and quiet here. She sketched Sylvia. She talked about the paintings she wanted to create.

'I wonder,' she said, 'if somewhere inside me there's still a memory of this place.'

She closed her eyes and squeezed them tight like she was trying to force a memory to break free.

'Maybe the baby's inside me still,' she said. 'But where could she be?'

She laughed.

'Hello, little baby,' she whispered. 'Can you hear me?'

Sylvia laughed.

'No,' said Mum. 'Not there. Nothing remembered at all.'

Then she leaned close to Sylvia and gasped as she looked into her eyes.

'But oh! I can certainly see the bonny little bairn in you!'

She drew baby Sylvia from memory, and Sylvia the little girl.

'Here you are!' she laughed.

The light faded. There were voices in the street. Sylvia went to the window and looked out. There were lights on in the social club, and its doors stood open. There'd be Wi-Fi there, maybe a phone signal.

'I could phone Maxine from there,' she said.

'Yes, you could.'

29

But what would she find in there? What kind of folk existed out here? She was shy.

'Come with me?' she said.

'Dressed like this?'

She came to join Sylvia at the window.

'Go on,' she said. 'I'm sure they'll be very welcoming.'

She stroked Sylvia's shoulders.

'It's OK. We'll both go another evening, eh?'

She couldn't sleep. She tried to read but the words were meaningless, black marks on white paper and nothing else. She had the scraper and the knife on the bedside table beside her. She dozed, drifting in and out of dreams. She crouched in long grass. There was the body of some creature below her. There was blood on it. She had the bloodied knife in her bloodied hand. Deep into the night, she woke and thought she heard the music again. She went to the window, tugged it open and leaned her head towards the night. The music had come and was now gone. In the village, a couple of house lights were still on. There was a tiny light from a distant farm. No moon. As she gazed upwards, she began to see stars between the stars, stars beyond the stars. To the south, there was a pale orange glow on the horizon. That must be Tyneside, that must be Newcastle, her home.

'Take me there,' she whispered.

The music started again, drew her back to the wilderness again. A weird jagged spiralling sound. It came from outside the village, she was sure of it, from the forest side. She stared into that deeper darkness.

Then she heard her name spoken.

'Sylvia. Sylvia.'

An insistent whisper rather than a call.

A whisper with a kind of laughter in it.

'Sylvia, look! I'm just down here.'

She looked down.

A boy, in the middle of the road, his pale hair illuminated by the stars, his pale face turned to her, his eyes shining where they caught the starlight too.

'Sylvia, it's me. It's Colin.'

He didn't need to shout. His words came smoothly, easily through the still night air.

'Why don't you come down, Sylvia? You could meet my brother.'

The music went on.

31

'That's him, Sylvia. Can you hear him? Why don't you come down?'

She couldn't go. Of course she couldn't go. She thought of the knife. She could go, take it with her, and that would give her some protection.

But no, of course she couldn't go.

And anyway, protection from what?

Then there was another figure, at the far end of the street. Another boy, walking easily towards them, taller, hair not so pale. He came to Colin's side. He ruffled Colin's hair. He looked up to Sylvia's window.

'Hello,' he said.

She didn't answer. She pulled back a few inches from the window.

'Take no notice of this nutter,' he said. 'Course she can't come down, you nit. Did I wake you up? Did you hear me playing?'

She didn't answer.

He put the flute or whistle or whatever it was to his mouth and played a few notes.

That strange music again. She wondered what instrument it was.

He held it up towards her.

'Do you want to see it?' he said.

She didn't answer. He laughed softly.

'I don't blame you,' he said. 'I wouldn't talk to me, either. Not when I turn up in the middle of the night.'

He played a few notes again.

'You could have a try some time, though,' he said.

He put his arm around his brother.

'Mebbe in the daytime. Come on, menace, it's time to get you home.'

He smiled up at her.

'Good night, Sylvia,' he said.

His eyes seemed filled with stars.

'My name's Gabriel,' he said.

They gazed at each other for a few more moments.

Then away the boys went, back towards the forest side.

Next morning, Mum was sticking some of Dad's photographs with Blu-tack to the kitchen wall.

Sylvia sat drinking tea.

Here they came: early photographs of seascapes, landscapes, townscapes. Waves crashing high over the pier wall at Tynemouth; misty morning with the flash of a kingfisher, fish in its beak; panoramas of the

Yorkshire Dales; great murmuration of starlings above Durham Cathedral; the lovely city, Newcastle, with its steep curved streets, its bridges and alleyways, a seal swimming in the river while a half-naked couple dances on the quayside above.

All of them so beautiful, so still.

A photograph, he used to tell her, *is a single instant caught in time.*

And think, he would tell her, *of how many instants there are in the whole of time.*

A photograph, he would say, *is a glimpse into eternity.*

She didn't have a clue what he was talking about, but she loved to look at them with him. They'd been made by him, his body was warm beside her, his voice was kind.

'Why,' she asked her mother this morning, 'are you doing this?'

'Maybe putting them out like this will help to keep him safe.'

'You said the other day you didn't even want to think about him.'

'Sometimes I don't . . . reckless man.'

There were more. Photographs of the three of them, of course. Photographs of Sylvia as she grew:

first scan of her in the womb, then a baby, an infant, a little girl, a teenager, her changing body, changing face, but all of the same person, instants of Sylvia caught in time.

Soon came the harsher ones, the more famous ones, the ones he'd been making during her teenage years.

His war photographs: bombed buildings, smashed statues, scorched corpses, weeping bloodied children; the young woman holding aside her veil to show the shattered face beneath.

'Why did he change?' whispered Sylvia.

But she knew the answers that he'd given, and the answers her mother gave now.

'By looking through a lens for so long, he said he'd grown up at last. He said he saw how things really were, how they always had been. He said there was a horror at the heart of it all, and it was his job to expose it.'

'That's not the truth,' said Sylvia. 'He should put the camera away. Or he should point it at me and Maxine and at the kids dancing, at kids protesting at the Monument. He's blind. He needs to learn from us. He's not grown up. The world's a better place than he thinks it is!'

Here came the photo that had been in all the

newspapers: Donovan Carr, in bulletproof vest and flak jacket, sitting among smoking steel ruins in Syria with a steel helmet on his head and a camera in his hand, and a smile on his face, like he had not a care in the world.

'Bonny man,' said Mum. 'Stupid, reckless man.'

Moments after that photo was taken, the airstrike came, an airstrike that was intended for another target. It almost killed him. It brought him a week in a hospital in Beirut, then a month in the Freeman Hospital in Newcastle, then months of psychotherapy and physiotherapy, and promises that he had learned his lesson, that he would steer clear of war zones. Empty promises. As soon as he was recuperated, he started searching for disaster once again.

Sylvia shuddered at the memory.

She shuddered at the memory of the rows there'd been.

He said that there was a kind of beauty in destruction, in war.

Her mum was reliving the same moments.

'Beauty in war!' she snapped now.

She set a jar of wild flowers on the shelf below the photographs.

'This is beauty,' she said. 'This is truth.'

She bent low to the flowers.

'Bring him back safe,' she whispered.

'So that you can tell him that you're leaving him?' said Sylvia.

'What?'

'You will, won't you?'

'I can't discuss that with my daughter.'

'Can't you? Why not? You want to leave him, don't you?'

Her mother turned away.

'Yes. No. Maybe. It isn't easy, Sylvia, being with a man who seeks destruction.'

Sylvia sighed. Yes, he seemed to seek destruction, but she also knew how proud she was of him. But like all so many so-called grown-ups, he needed to change. He needed to learn from the young.

'Maxine! *Maxine*! It's you!'

Later that day. She'd come higher than she had so far. She was standing on a crag. When she stood on tiptoe, she was sure she could see as far as the sea. That must be it, that flat dark edge on the horizon below the empty blue.

And the phone. Somehow, up here, it worked.

'Maxine!'

'Yes, it's me,' answered Maxine. 'Who else would it be?'

'The signal fades, Maxine. Tell me *everything*!'

'Well . . . Where do I start?'

'Everything!'

'You sound desperate. You've only been there a couple of days.'

'I'm fine. I'm getting used to it. Tell me. Tell me. Tell me quick.'

'Well . . . the gig went well. Mickey was brilliant, of course –' her voice faded, crackled, went away, came back again – 'and afterwards all back to mine . . .'

'To yours?'

'. . . all night, talking, drinking . . .'

'Who?'

The signal faded.

Sylvia moved about the crag, seeking the signal. Waved the phone, a wand.

No signal.

She pointed the phone at the horizon and took a photograph.

The signal came back.

'. . . and all today to Cullercoats Bay and . . .'

Then gone. Just nothing.

'Maxine! Maxine!'

Waved the wand, picked up the silence.

'I'll send you a photo,' she said.

Clicked *send*.

She tried again, again.

Nothing. Nada. Absence. Nowt.

'Damn place!' she yelled.

She yelled again. Filled her lungs with the huge northern air and howled it out again.

So wonderful to howl like this, to fill the empty air with sound, with herself, with the yell of Sylvia Carr.

She stamped her feet.

Thud thud. Thump thump. Crack crack. Stamp stamp.

She laughed out loud, as loud as it was possible to be: the gorgeousness of noise just pouring out of her. She screamed and yelled, a beast. So great to have the freedom of it, to yell and not be heard except by the buzzards and the sheep and the scuttling, shifting, buzzing things inside the heather and the grass. So great in that moment not to be in the city at all, but to be alone out here, in this vast and empty wilderness.

'I am Sylvia!' she yelled, to that vastness and that

wilderness. 'I am a howling beast! This is me!'

And then just wordless screams and howls and giggling, until she was all yelled out and grinning at herself and her frantic heart now settling again.

And there she was, standing alone on the high crag, and saying to herself, 'Sylvia, you are. You're bliddy mental, pet.'

Then she caught her breath and crouched down to touch the dark rock beneath her feet. There was moss and lichen growing there, but there were markings too. Grooves carved into the rock, curves and circles and whirls and linked spirals. She ran her hands across the patterns, traced them with her fingers.

The marks swirled beneath her gaze.

'Weird place,' she whispered. 'Weird as bliddy Sylvia Carr.'

She kept on touching, following the patterns, so strange, so lovely.

Her head reeled.

The phone buzzed.

A message from Maxine.

Hell's teeth, Sylvia, it's so bleak! So empty!

Back down over the moor she walked. The swirling and shuddering inside her went on. There was a family of deer on a far fell. They stood still a moment to watch, then strolled on, unconcerned, at ease in this, their world. She looked towards the forest's bulk. There it was, so heavy, so dense, mile after mile after mile of it. All of the trees so uniform and dark. They undulated with the land, broken only by the reservoir, the lake, which from this distance lay still and dark and dead as stone.

There came another of those muffled booms she'd heard the day before. Nothing, she told herself. Illusion.

She snapped some grass. She blew a high-pitched note and yes, a curlew cried.

There were skylarks high up, so high and tiny they could hardly be seen. Their song sang her back to Newcastle, to the town moor, the wide and lovely grassy space so near to the city's heart. Just last week, she'd sat below the singing skylarks on a green steel bench. The afternoon was warm. She linked arms with Maxine and leaned against her. They whispered together of what they might do as they grew older, when they'd left school, moved out into the world.

They knew they couldn't really know, but they shivered with the thrill of it, the fright of it.

'What if there is no world at all?' they said.

They were filled with dread and doubt.

They muttered about the burning planet, about hunger and war and death, and about dreadful adults who failed and kept on failing. They talked about how different it must have been when their parents were young. They clenched their fists and talked about the protests they'd gone on and the protests still to come. They edged for a second close to despair. But the sun was beautiful as it fell down over the lovely moor, and the skylarks' song was wonderful, and their bodies close against each other were familiar and comforting and beautiful too, and they had friends close by, and families, and their minds raced, and their hearts beat and their souls soared as high as the larks that went on singing over them. And they were young, and despite all doubts and all the horrors, they ached with love and friendship for each other, they ached with the desire to help create a better world.

'Will you always stay here?' said Maxine. 'Will you leave, will you go wandering like he did?'

'Lots of us will leave,' said Sylvia, 'and we'll be

scattered across the earth. But we'll stay in each other's hearts, and we'll hear each other's song, wherever we are, forever and forever.'

Now, in far Northumberland, she held her hand against the sun and tried to see the birds, and did: jet black dots that hovered high over her head, high over their nests scraped into the earth, and they sang, and sang.

'Hello, skylarks!' she called.

'Sing my song to Maxine,' she called. 'Sing Maxine's song to me.'

And here came another distant jet, and another in its wake, such dreadful things that streaked so silently through the gorgeous sky.

She waved clenched fists at them.

She flung an invisible knife at them.

She fired an imaginary bazooka at them.

She yelled curses at them.

And as she yelled, they curved and turned, as if they'd seen and heard, and this was their answer, and here they came, arrowing at her, black and pointed and weirdly beautiful things, so low she felt she might almost reach up to touch them, and she stood with her curses still pouring from her, and her fists still raised, until the air was shattered by their roar and the earth around her quaked and she had to bend low, to protect her ears, protect her yearning soul.

Saturday night. It was music night. Sylvia said she didn't want to go. Boring ancient music, she said. Boring ancient people. Boring ancient place. And she wanted to read, or to write, or to draw, or just to stay in the house and feel miserable or think about the world or about the beauty of skylarks or about being young or about missing Maxine and about wanting to protest or to go to Cullercoats Bay.

And her mother just smiled.

'Ah, Sylvia,' she said. 'I know you when you're feeling shy.'

Sylvia scowled and flushed.

'It'll do us good, love,' she said. 'Be nice to meet more neighbours, won't it?'

Sylvia grunted. But she put on clean jeans, put on a jumper, put on some star-shaped earrings, put some lipstick on.

'That's better,' said her mother. 'What a bonny lass you are!'

She stood beside her, put her arm around her, turned

them both so that they saw each other arm-in arm in the mirror on the wall close to the photographs.

'What a bonny *pair* of lasses we are!' she said.

Despite herself, Sylvia smiled.

She saw her face in her mother's, her mother's face in hers.

Out they went, along the little street through the fading light towards the wide-open doors of the community club.

A man strode past them with a violin case strapped to his back.

He said good evening. Her mother said good evening back.

There were a few others, folk of all ages, carrying instruments and cases. They walked in from the places outside the village, one or two emerged from the dark forest itself. And there were vans and cars. And some kids on bicycles with clogs dangling from their backs.

They went through the door.

Sylvia bit her lip. She was shy, shy.

There was a long bar, men and women standing at it drinking pints of beer, glasses of wine. Groups of folk were sitting at square tables. Some kids running about and skipping in the empty space at the far end of the room. Garish strip lights on the ceiling. Sylvia kept her head down, didn't like such light, that could expose so clearly her blushing face.

She stood at the bar with her mother, who ordered wine and peanuts.

'What would you like?' she asked Sylvia.

Vodka, thought Sylvia.

'Nothing,' she said. 'A coke.'

'Find a place?'

'Hello, Sylvia.'

It was Andreas Muller. He was at a nearby table, glass of beer before him. Another man and woman with him.

'You'll come and sit with us?' said Andreas.

Sylvia hesitated, then her mum was with her and they went together to sit there.

The others were a farmer and his wife from a farm on a distant fell. They introduced themselves as Oliver and Daphne Dodd. The man was in a brown tweed suit. The woman wore an old red-and-brown floral dress. She had a tiny flute with her that she told them was a piccolo.

'Do you play anything?' Oliver asked her.

Sylvia shook her head. Nothing, though she

suddenly remembered the recorder lessons with Miss Pringle at primary school, the feel of the plastic mouthpiece against her lips, her fingers on the fingerholes, the awkwardness she felt in playing it, the uncertain notes that came out.

She swigged her coke. Her mum squeezed her arm and talked to Andreas and the others about the club, the village, the beauty of the place. Andreas said that she had returned after a long separation. Oliver and Daphne asked about her life. She told them of her work dealing with troubled kids.

'There's many of them these days,' said Daphne. 'But maybe it's always been so. The world has always been a marvellous and troubled place.'

She turned her eyes to Sylvia.

'Are you a troubled bairn, my love?'

Sylvia blushed and looked away.

Her mother touched her arm.

'Just shy,' she said.

And the word made Sylvia flare inside herself.

She wanted to snap, 'I am not shy!'

She wanted to snap, 'And if I'm shy, so *what*?'

She wanted to report the lovely words that Maxine said:

'You're not shy, my lovely friend. What looks like shyness is your strength. You are open and honest and true and brave.'

The thought of Maxine calmed her down.

'The ones to worry about,' she wanted to say, 'are those who are not shy at all.'

The adults had moved on. Daphne and Oliver tried to remember Sylvia's grandparents, but they could not place them.

'It was so long ago,' said Daphne. 'There were so many of you. We remember the days of you all moving away.'

Sylvia listened half-heartedly and swigged her coke.

She thought of her life in Newcastle, of her lovely friends.

People played separate tunes on separate fiddles. A couple of kids made squeaks on strange little bagpipes. A young redhaired woman stood in a corner, eyes closed, a set of the bagpipes strapped to her waist. She squeezed the bellows against her body with her elbow. She ran her fingers over the narrow pipes and bird-like notes came out.

A couple of girls clattered on the floor with their clogs.

A tall man started to set up a microphone in the empty space.

'Hello, Sylvia.'

It was Colin, standing close at her side.

'We're glad you've come,' he said.

He pointed across the tables. Gabriel was there, with another boy and a girl. They each held fiddles at their shoulders and played a tune together. Gabriel paused in his playing and grinned and waved.

'Come and sit with us if you can,' said Colin. 'I'm Colin,' he said to Sylvia's mother. 'That's my brother Gabriel. My dad's here somewhere too. Hello, Andreas.'

Andreas smiled. 'Hello, my friend,' he said.

And Colin was gone.

Sylvia's mother smiled, squeezed Sylvia's arm again.

'I met them when I was out,' murmured Sylvia.

She swigged her coke.

Andreas laughed. 'Nobody comes to Blackwood these days without coming across our Colin.'

Sylvia looked towards Gabriel. He leaned forward as he practised with his violin. His body swayed. She couldn't make out the tune he played. He paused again and looked back at her. She looked away.

The tall man at the microphone called out, 'Good

evening, you canny folk. Good to have your presence in this bonny place.'

Oliver said that the man's name was Mike.

He sang a song filled with slaughter and death and pain.

He laughed.

'Aye, the old ballads, eh? Ancient tales of bloody slaughter and savage death. But here's a lovely one for the tender-hearted.'

And he sang again, of forests and fells and wind and birdsong and flowing water.

Then others stepped up with their fiddles and whistles and accordions and pipes. At first there were those who were clearly just learning. They were awkward with their instruments. Their tunes were stilted, marred by mistakes but the people in the room urged them on, applauded them. Then others came. Old men and women played for them. Gabriel and his friends played a dance tune on their fiddles that had everyone clapping their hands and stamping their feet in time. When it was over, Gabriel held his fiddle high and laughed towards Sylvia. Again she looked away.

Sylvia swigged her coke and tried to resist. She tried to tell herself that this was ancient stuff, stupid stuff. But the music kept touching her, moving into her. The garish lights were dimmed. She started to relax, to move past her shyness and her resistance, to give herself up to what was going on. An old man, old as Andreas, dressed in a dusty brown suit, played a set of pipes as if they were part of his own body, as if the music from them was the music of his own breath. The room was hushed as he played. When he stopped, it was as if they had been released from a spell. Other pipers, other accordion players. Sylvia's attention weaved in and out. At moments, she saw Gabriel looking across the room at her. At moments, she told herself how silly this all was. She couldn't be so moved by stuff like this. But again and again she was drawn back in. She forgot about Gabriel. Again and again she had the sense that this music was seeking her, that it wanted her to abandon herself to it.

'Are you OK, love?' whispered her mum at one point.

Sylvia had almost forgotten that she was there.

'Yes,' she muttered. 'Yes.'

Her mother smiled, widened her eyes.

'Makes you feel so inadequate, doesn't it?' she said.

Sylvia nodded.

'Yes.'

'Should have kept on with that old recorder, eh?'

Daphne went to the microphone, played her piccolo. A weird jaunty, dancy tune that somehow caused them all to laugh. The young red-haired woman played her pipes. Her playing ached with yearning and lamentation. She closed her eyes as she played. Sylvia stared. It was as if the woman had somehow disappeared, as if she had become the pipes, become the music. Sylvia groaned as a clog dancer stepped up to join her. *No, don't spoil it!* she thought to herself. But the deep and weird insistent thuds that the clogs made on the floor were drumbeats calling down into the earth itself, an insistent beat below the sweetness of the pipes, and the thuds vibrated on Sylvia's body, travelled deep into Sylvia's mind.

She looked at Gabriel again. Now he stood at the side of the room with his friends. He gazed at the players, not at her. His body swayed as if in a dance. Sylvia watched him. His body, so rhythmical. Then came a pair of girls younger than she was. They stood together and sang in beautiful harmony about meadows and mornings and fish and birds and mothers and fathers and bairns, and tears came to Sylvia's eyes as she watched them there, so in tune with each other, so bound to each other in the beauty of the song and the beauty of themselves, and she thought of Maxine again, and she leaned to her mother to feel their bodies close and her mother put her arm around her and hummed along to the ancient familiar tune until it was done and everyone in the room cheered and clapped and then Mike came to the microphone to thank them all again and he raised his arms high and said, 'So now, you fine and bonny folk, let us get on with our drinking and let us dance!'

And he stepped aside and a new band gathered in the empty space and they set quick music going and folk began to dance.

Andreas leaned across the table towards her.

'Do you play?' he asked.

Just the recorder, and very badly, she almost said: that thing that had seemed so ridiculous and alien to her. But she simply shook her head.

'Perhaps you will come to,' he said.

She shrugged.

'Do you dance?' he asked.

Dance? Yes, she could dance with Maxine, with Francesca and Mickey, and yes, she could feel the music flowing into her now, feel her muscles and limbs responding to it. But how could she dance here, with these unfamiliar people in this strange new place?

She lowered her eyes, shook her head.

'Mrs Carr?' he asked.

Her mother laughed. 'It would be a pleasure, Andreas. You'll be OK, darling?'

Sylvia nodded, and she watched the ancient frail man and the fit young woman move through the tables towards the dancing space. Andreas held her mother's waist and hand. They moved stiffly together to the tune.

'Hello, Sylvia.'

It was Gabriel at her side, violin case in his hand.

'You want to dance?' he said.

She shook her head.

'It's not hard. It's nothing to be scared about.'

She just looked back at him. Why would he think she was scared?

'Hello, Gabriel,' said Daphne. 'Sylvia's OK. She'll dance if she wants to, son.'

'I know,' he said. 'Can I sit down?'

Sylvia shrugged. He sat down. He picked at the bowl of peanuts on the table. He rested his violin case beside them.

The farmer took his wife by her hand.

'You've got company now,' he said to Sylvia, 'so if you would not mind, I will lead my wife away and dance with her.'

And hand-in-hand Oliver and Daphne went to the dance.

'They're magic, eh?' said Gabriel.

'Aye.'

'How you settling in here?' said Gabriel.

Sylvia looked towards her mum, who waved.

'You don't say much, do you?' he said.

She still felt the echoes of the clog dancer inside her.

Why should she say *anything* to him?

She put a peanut into her mouth.

'I kind of knew you'd come,' he said.

'Aye? How's that?'

'It's weird. But I did. When I saw you at the window, I thought, Sylvia was bound to come. Is that stupid?'

'Probably.'

He leaned closer, as if there was something urgent pushing him towards her.

'The world's bloody awful, isn't it?' he said. 'But it isn't, is it? It's bloody awful and it isn't bloody awful. It's bloody marvellous.'

She said nothing.

'Sorry,' he said. 'Maybe I've been on my own up here too long.'

She popped another peanut in her mouth.

'Aye,' she said. 'Maybe you have been.'

'Would you come outside with me?'

'What?'

'Just a few moments. I'm not weird. Or not weird in a way that's horrible-weird.'

She looked towards the dancing space.

She saw her mum happily dancing.

'We'll stay in the light,' he said. 'Just a few moments. I've got something I want to show you.'

'*What*?'

He put his hand across his face.

'Oh hell, no. I'm so stupid. Tell me to clear off. I'll just go away.'

She laughed. He looked so embarrassed. She said OK and she stood up. The door to outside wasn't far away. It was open to the night. She led him through it.

There were already a few people outside. A little group gossiping together. A couple of blokes smoking cigarettes. A couple kissing. No one seemed to notice them. There was a steel bench at the edge of the light. They went to sit on it. The music poured through the doors after them into the night, into their bodies and minds.

Gabriel put his violin case on his lap. He looked around to check nobody was looking. He opened it. He reached beneath his violin. He took out what looked like a small flute.

'This is it,' he said. 'What I was playing the other night.'

He held it in his hands. Cream-coloured, a few inches long.

'It's called a hollow bone,' he said.

He held it towards her.

'It's the bone of an animal,' he said.

'A *bone*?'

'Yes. Maybe it's from a deer. Maybe a fox. Some are made from birds or even fish.'

She recoiled. How could she put *that* in her hands?

'See the mouthpiece?' he said. 'See the finger holes? It's been turned into an instrument.'

He held it out again.

'I don't know how old,' he said. 'Maybe a hundred years, maybe many hundreds more. Or maybe only five or ten. Take it. Hold it. It won't harm you.'

Still, she couldn't, though there was enough light for

her to see the weird beauty in it. She touched it with the tip of her index finger. It was smooth, dry. A gentle curve to it.

'I haven't shown it to anybody else,' he said. 'Well, just to Colin, and Dad, but since it brought you to the window . . .'

He put it to his lips and played a single wavering note.

'They were the first kind of musical instruments,' he said. 'They were used in ancient caves. They've been found all around the world.'

He played a few more soft, hardly-audible notes.

'They were magical objects,' he said. 'They were used to charm the living. They were used to call the dead.'

She felt the notes flowing through her.

'This is where all the music started,' he said.

Someone nearby said, 'What the hell is that?'

He stopped playing.

'Isn't there *something*?' he said. 'Isn't there something powerful and strange?'

Don't stop, she wanted to say.

'Maybe when I was playing the hollow bone here in the north,' he said, 'you heard me from the city's heart.'

Sylvia's mother came out of the door.

Gabriel slipped the hollow bone back into the case.

'You OK out here?' said Mum.

'Aye,' said Sylvia.

'You're Gabriel, aren't you?'

'Yes,' said Gabriel.

He shook hands with her.

Her mother was happy, maybe a little tipsy.

'It's so lovely, love!' she said. 'I'm making so many friends. Gabriel, I met your dad. And isn't he a lovely *dancer*? Oh, just look at those stars!'

The music played on inside. She swayed and tapped her feet.

'Are you two not coming in to dance?' she said.

'Maybe later, Mum.'

'Ah, well, I'd best get back inside if you're all right out here.'

She left them.

'She's nice,' said Gabriel.

'What did you mean, I heard you from the city's heart?'

'I don't know.' He rocked his head as if to show how stupid he was. 'There's so much I don't know. There's so much that everybody doesn't know. What brought you here?'

'My mum had had enough of work. She'd had enough of my dad. She needed somewhere peaceful and beautiful. That's all.'

'But you. Why did *you* come?'

'I didn't want to come at all!'

She laughed at herself. He laughed.

'And now you're here,' he said.

'And now I'm here.'

'And it isn't too bad after all.'

She looked into his shining eyes.

She shrugged.

'It's not *quite* as bad as I thought.'

They listened to the music that came from inside. People moved in and out of the door. Several greeted Gabriel. He introduced Sylvia and they greeted her too.

'There's a whole far-flung community,' he said, 'scattered across the moors and the fells. Music draws them together.'

A bunch of kids squatted on the grass, murmuring together. They swigged a bottle of something.

'Maybe we should go back in,' said Sylvia.

She got up and went to the door.

Pipers and fiddlers were playing.

Gabriel came to her side. Their parents were hand-in-hand, twisting and spiralling as they danced.

'Doesn't look like anybody needs us,' said Gabriel.

They backed away again.

'Will you come further?' said Gabriel.

'Further?'

'Too many folk about here. Just a little bit further.'

He nodded towards the darkness between the village and the forest.

'There's another bench, further out. It's OK. You know I'm OK, don't you? Just a bit crazy, that's all.'

They went into the shadows. There was laughter from behind them. Sylvia's heart was thumping. The grass they walked on sparkled. The edge of the forest was stark, pitch-black. They came to the bench and sat on it. There was still light from the moon and the stars. Light from the door of the club was like a distant lantern.

He took out the hollow bone again.

'They were used in initiation rites,' he said. 'They helped children to go through the transformations that would turn them into adults.'

Gabriel laughed softly. His eyes sparkled, his face gleamed.

'You think I'm talking crap,' he said.

'No,' she said, but she didn't understand.

'What do we do with kids today? Stuff them into schools, trap them between four walls, cram them and test them. Where are the rites of passage now? GCSEs? A Levels?'

'I've got GCSEs next term!' She laughed. 'I should be back at home swotting for them now.'

'You're better off out here.'

'Am I?'

'Something's wrong, isn't it? Look at the state of the bliddy world. Look at all the anxious, troubled kids. We need more, don't we?'

'More *what*?'

'More of everything! Oh, I don't know! I don't know nothing!'

Then he was intense again.

'Do you not *feel* it?' he said.

'Feel what?'

'The need to be the real you, the need to be the Sylvia Carr that all of creation wants you to be?'

She started to say that no she didn't, but she faltered. Was that what the yearning inside her was? To be the person that all of creation wanted her to be?

She looked into this strange boy's eyes. There was a spirit burning in him, there was a passion as he looked back into her eyes.

'You're special,' he said. 'You're different.'

'Oh, aye? You don't even know me. You've only just met me.'

'That doesn't matter. You've got a soul or something. I don't bloody know but I can see it in you. Something we've lost. Something we need. Something we haven't got the words for.'

'Ballocks,' she said.

He laughed.

'Aye,' he said softly. 'Mebbe I have been out here alone too long. Mebbe it is just total ballocks, but I look at you and I think you're somebody special.'

'I'm just me. Little Sylvia. Sylvia Carr.'

He stared into the night like he was searching for something in it.

'That's it!' he whispered. 'Mebbe you're the thing that I've been trying to be but can't be.'

'And what's that, Gabriel?'

'Some kind of shaman or something.'

'Eh?'

'A shaman. A magician. A magic-worker.'

'Oh aye?'

'Aye! Somebody who goes into the darkness and the wilderness and transforms themselves and then comes out into the world again with spells and music that'll change the whole world.'

She laughed.

'I know,' he said. 'What a barmy notion! But just imagine! Mebbe it's true.'

She giggled.

'Aye. Mebbe it is, Gabriel.'

He gasped.

'Yes!' he said.

'Yes what?'

'You'll need your own.'

'My own what?'

'Your own hollow bone, Sylvia!'

She stared at him, this weird boy she was with on a bench at the edge of the pitch-black forest. What the hell was going on?

'We'll find you one!' he said. 'We'll *make* you one!'

'You're mad,' she whispered.

'I know,' said Gabriel. 'And so are you.'

That night when she woke up, or when she thought she woke up, she heard the music again. But as she lay there, she knew that it wasn't coming from outside this time, but somehow from inside herself. She was the hollow bone. Something was playing her. She opened her mouth and let a note come out. She felt happy. A breeze was playing softly on her window. An owl was calling. She let the note come out. She thought of the illuminated city beyond the horizon, the dark forest at the end of the street. She relaxed into the strange and ordinary knowledge that her mind was so huge, that it could contain such space, such distance, that it could include the galaxies above her and curlews and owls and steel benches and hollow bones. She breathed out gentle notes again. They came easily from her lungs, her throat, her open lips. Tomorrow, she'd go back to where the marks on the rocks were, where there was a signal. She'd find Maxine's voice there, she'd find Maxine's ear.

'Aha! A boy! So that's what all the fuss is!'

'Oh, Maxine!'

'. . . handsome?'

'What?'

'Come on, Sylvia. Is he hot?'

'I guess so.'

'You *guess* so? Nice name. *Gabriel.*'

'Yes.'

Crackle crackle.

She waved the phone about.

'. . . doing all the way up *there*?'

'What?'

'What's he doing all the way . . . ?'

The signal faded, came back again.

'I don't know.'

'*You.* You don't *know.* What you like?'

'I'm seeing him today.'

'Aha! That's good. That's very good!'

'What's happening? What you doing?'

Crackle crackle. Fade, fade.

'. . . Saturday morning.'

'Eh?'

'. . . lying down on the Tyne Bridge on Saturday morning.'

'Good!'

'. . . riding slow bikes through the Tyne . . .'

'Through the Tyne?'

'Tyne Tunnel, you nit!'

Crackle crackle.

She waved the phone about, a wand. Stamped her feet on the rock markings as if that would help.

'Find out.'

'What about?'

'About *him*. Then tell—'

The signal went. She stamped the rock and waved the wand but couldn't get it back.

'Bye, bye, Maxine,' she whispered to the air.

She sat down on the rock. She tightened the laces of her walking boots and grinned. They were so comfortable. She took a blade of grass and blew and a curlew called. The skylarks sang. There were no jets. She lay back on the rock, on the weird patternings. She imagined the patterns being impressed into the skin of her shoulders and back. She wriggled, told herself she could feel that happening. She let the light of the sun fall down on her. High above, a pair of buzzards slowly wheeled. She closed her eyes and let their frail, high-pitched cries come into her.

Gabriel. She knew she'd never met anyone like him. Yes, he was handsome, he was bonny. It was something more than that. It was the thing that burned from his eyes. Passion, or spirit, or what he'd said about her. Soul. Or was it what he said it was, a kind of madness.

That afternoon, they'd said. That's when they'd meet.

She didn't know why, but she took the scraper and the knife. She wrapped them in an old T-shirt and put it into her little rucksack. Her mum had made some sandwiches for her. She gave her a bottle of water.

'Never go without supplies,' she said. 'Not out here.'

They looked at the map of where they were: the village, the moors, the forest, the farms, the paths and bridleways, the streams. Crossed swords to show where battles had been. Gothic writing to show the most ancient places. Crosses to show antiquities.

Sylvia traced her tracks out of the village.

'That's where I was this morning,' she said. 'There's lots of weird markings on the rocks up there.'

'Rock art,' said her mum. 'Lots of it round here. Nobody knows what it means or how it was made but it'll last for ever more. And there's marks like it all around the world.'

There was a broad area with a jagged red border

around it and bold red capitals:

DANGER AREA

'What's that?' she said.

Her mum groaned.

'That's the military zone. It's where the army tests its guns and shells. Where the soldiers play their war games. Out here, in all this loveliness.'

'That's what it was,' said Sylvia.

'What?'

'I heard explosions. Thought I was dreaming them.'

Her mum laughed bitterly.

'They're real enough. How else can they make sure that everything works? That everything's so accurate?'

She waved her hand across the map.

'It's forever the same,' said her mum. 'The land looks so peaceful, but that's the lie. There are ancient battle sites everywhere.'

She pointed at the crossed swords.

'There and there and there and there,' she said.

She mimed pinching a piece of the map and peeling it away.

'Lift up the heather. Lift up the grass. Clear the soil.

We'd find centuries of bones beneath.'

She opened her fingers, as if to let it fall again.

'All gone, all covered over, all hidden again.'

She folded the map.

'You won't get lost. His dad said he knows the place like the back of his hand. The weather's fine. You like Gabriel?'

Sylvia shrugged.

Her mother smiled.

'I've got a sense there might be a lot to him. Where will you go?'

'He just said he'd show me around.'

'Good. Don't go too far. Back before dark, yes?'

'Yes, mum.'

'Good lass. Got your phone?'

'Aye. Not that it'll be any good.'

She sat on a hard kitchen chair with her boots and her waterproof on and her little rucksack on her back. She chewed her lips and stared at the wall. Her heart was quick.

Her mum giggled.

'You look like you did on the first day of school, Sylvia!'

'Do I?'

'Yes. Being a very good girl, and being a bit scared.'

She heard him coming through the gate, heard his knock at the door.

Her mum kissed her brow, told her to have fun.

She smiled as she guided Sylvia to the door.

He walked with her past the abandoned chapel, past the club.

'Where to, then?' he said.

'You're the one that knows the way.'

'Gulp! Am I? The way to where?'

She shrugged and laughed.

'This way, then,' he said.

The roadway turned into a rough cinder track. There was an abandoned wheel-less sports car at its edge. There were three collapsed totem poles lying in long grass.

'They were made by the foresters years ago,' he told her. 'They turned rotten and had to come down.'

They were cross-shaped. There were carvings and markings on them: beasts and mask-like faces; wings.

'Kids used to dance round them,' he said. 'People had picnics under them. This is where I was playing when you heard me.'

'Why at night?'

'More exciting, isn't it? Don't you like to do things at night?'

Aye, she did. Of course she did.

'And out here, you can tell yourself that you can see the ghosts rising.'

'Aye?'

'Aye! A whole crowd of them climbed out of the ground a couple of weeks back!'

Ghosts. When she was a little girl, lying in bed, she was terrified by the thought of them shifting in the shadows or knocking at her window.

'They say they're making new ones to replace them,' said Gabriel.

'New ghosts?'

'New totem poles, nit.'

'Good. Kids need things to dance around.'

Sylvia crouched beside them. Tiny ferns were growing from the carvings. There were patches of bright green moss. She saw beetles and snails and spider webs. The timber was crumbling away where the poles once joined the earth and was turning to earth itself. She pressed her palms to the wood. As it decayed, new life and beauty was growing and gathering on it.

They walked on. There was a broad fast-running stream with soft turf and rocks at its edge. A woman was there with her baby. She crouched down, holding the baby's hands, shuffling backwards. The baby walked, tottered, fell, stood again, walked, tottered, fell.

The woman giggled.

'Come on, Rosie,' she laughed. 'You can do it, my lovely!'

She saw them there.

'Hello, Gabriel!' she said. 'Look, Rosie, there's Gabriel and his friend! Show them how you walk!'

The baby walked, tottered, fell on to her backside and sat there grinning.

Sylvia grinned back. There was a photograph of her first early steps in the kitchen, her dad holding her hands high and laughing as she rose and tumbled and rose again.

The woman laughed, filled with delight.

'This is Sylvia,' said Gabriel. 'This is Isabel.'

They greeted each other.

'Wave to Sylvia!' said Isabel, and Rosie waved and laughed and wiggled her bottom as if in a dance.

On they went. Across a stone bridge with timber

handrails. There were fish in the water below.

'Trout,' said Gabriel.

A large grey heron rose into the sky from further down the stream.

They played Pooh sticks, dropping their sticks from one side of the bridge, turning to the other side to see which came through first.

'I won! I won!' said Sylvia.

'No, you didn't. That was my stick!'

'No, it wasn't! Come on. Again!'

They laughed into each other's eyes.

They played again and again for a little while, then went on.

At the edge of the forest, Isabel called.

'Rosie's waving bye-bye!'

They turned. Isabel was standing on the bank, holding Rosie high.

They waved back.

'Bye-bye, Rosie!' they called.

Gabriel touched her elbow for a moment, and they both turned away from the child and followed the narrow track into the trees.

Into the shade. Into the sudden muffling of sound. The trees dead straight, dead vertical, dead tall, planted in dead straight rows. Little sunlight fell down through them.

Sylvia frowned. Long ago tales of Goldilocks came to her, of red Riding Hood, Snow White.

'When I was little,' she found herself saying, 'we went to Chopwell Wood for a Christmas tree. I cried all the time. Thought the bears were coming for us.'

'Some want them back again,' he said.

'Bears? Here?'

'Mebbe not bears. But wolves, maybe, and definitely the lynx. That'll be coming soon. No reason for it not to. There'd be no real danger, not to us.'

They went further in. Sylvia tried to imagine the lynx and the wolf in the shadow and light between the trees.

'That'd be great,' she said.

'Aye. But we need to put the wolf and the lynx inside ourselves as well. It's no good rewilding the world if we don't rewild ourselves.'

They moved on in silence.

She found herself thinking of herself as a forest.

The lynx prowled inside her.

The wolf howled at the fringes of her imagination.

She imagined herself turning from Sylvia to a beast.

She padded through this forest on all fours, looking for prey, nervous of becoming prey herself.

She shaped her mouth as if to snuffle, to whimper, to howl.

She imagined the forest darkening, darkening.

The forest was filled with all these tales, these images, these possibilities.

Now she was Gretel, with Hansel at her side, about to get lost.

She glanced back to where they'd come from. Would they ever be able to find their way out again?

She laughed at herself.

Stop being mental, she said to herself.

Then she checked herself.

No, she told herself. *Don't stop yourself. Be mental, Sylvia.*

They left the main path and walked on along a narrower hardly-visible pathway through the trees. She stumbled on the uneven earth. There were roots and fallen fir cones, great gouges in the surface from the time of planting. She looked at the disturbed earth, seeking ancient scrapers and blades among the soil and stones.

They came to a clearing: mossy earth, mossy stones, a little hawthorn tree with white blossom shining on it. A dark pool with bright green weed on it. Dappled sunlight falling into it.

They sat on stones. There were insects buzzing. A tiny froglet hopped and squirmed between blades of grass.

'There's places like this all through the forest,' said Gabriel. 'Some folk don't know that they're here at all. Old forgotten places. Remnants of how the place was before all these heavy trees were planted.'

If her mind was a forest, she thought, were there clearings like this in her mind, remnants of ancient Sylvias?

He took the hollow bone from his rucksack. He started to play. A long sweet breathy note came out.

'You have to blow really gently at first,' he said, 'to get the feeling for it, to learn how to get the proper vibration going.'

He blew again.

'Look,' he whispered. 'Squirrels.'

Yes, there were two red squirrels on a branch not too high above. And crows in the branches higher above.

'You're going to tell me you called them, aren't you?' she said.

'Aye, course I did. I played and they arrived. You saw that. What else would you like to see?'

He played again. He gasped and grinned and pointed through the trees.

'There!' he said. 'See it?'

'See what?'

'There, look! There. Ah, it's gone. Your turn now.'

He held it towards her.

He wiped the mouthpiece on his shirt then held it out again.

'It won't bite you,' he said.

She took it.

It was so light. Not much broader than a finger, a bit longer than a hand. Three finger holes. So strange to hold it.

Could she raise it to her lips? What part of what beast was it? Where had it been? Who else had held it? What other lips had touched it? What diseases might it carry?

'Where did it come from?' she asked.

'I was out on my own, not long after we moved here. I wanted to explore everything. Found a farmhouse all in ruins miles out on the fells. One of the dozens of farmhouses that have been abandoned. There were still chairs in there, still a couple of pictures on the walls, ancient cooker in the kitchen. Doors dangling, roof all fallen in. There was a mossy heap of old cutlery and crockery and light fittings and stuff. Found it in there. Just lying in all the rubbish. Didn't know what it was at first, then found out about such things. Hollow bones, the first musical instruments. The kind of thing that shamans and magicians once used. Maybe the farmer or his wife was a shaman or magician. No reason why not.'

She thought of Oliver and Daphne Dodd at the music night. The woman in an old floral dress playing the piccolo. Yes, no reason why she might not be a magician.

'All music was magic,' said Gabriel. 'All song was a spell. When the magician played the hollow bone, they merged with beasts and birds. Play the bone of an eagle and you became the eagle. The bone of a fox and you became the fox. Play it well enough, and you cross the borders between the living and the dead.'

He peered at the hollow bone.

'And do you play it well enough?' she asked.

'No. I don't know what animal it came from. And when I play it, I'm just me, Gabriel. Nothing changes. And I stay in this place. Just here. My brain gets in the way.'

'Your brain?'

'I can't stop thinking. I can't stop analysing. I'm too clever. I can't just give myself up to it.'

He laughed.

'You think I'm mad, but the real truth is I'm just not mad enough. Mebbbe you are, though. Mebbe you'll call out the beasts. Mebbe you'll become a beast. Maybe you'll get through to the spirit world.'

'Ha!'

'Go on, Sylvia. Play it.'

She held the hollow bone before her face.

'It won't harm you,' he said.

'Won't it?'

She raised it to her lips and took it away again.

Her hands were trembling.

She raised it again. She breathed gently into it.

Nothing. Just the intensified sound of her nervous breath.

'You'll feel when it starts to work,' he said.

'Relax,' he said. 'Imagine the sound and that'll help to create the sound.'

She closed her eyes. She rested a finger on one of the finger holes. She breathed, and yes, she began to hear and feel how her breath could be turned to music. She covered another fingerhole. She breathed harder. She found the note again and held it for a second, another second, another second.

It made her dizzy, dreamy.

She breathed the notes. Her lips and tongue tingled with the vibrations.

She lowered the hollow bone, opened her eyes.

Gabriel was grinning.

She giggled back at him.

'Hell's teeth!' she said.

'You'll always be able to find the note now.'

She wiped her lips.

She looked at the thing in her hands.

'Do it again, Sylvia.'

She breathed again, found the note more easily this time. Found the way to play a little louder. Found out how to change the note by using the fingerholes. Began to find out how to take control. She felt the notes inside herself as well as hearing them outside herself. Closed her eyes, relaxed into the music.

'There!' said Gabriel.

He pointed through the trees.

'See?' he said.

Sylvia caught her breath.

A deer, and another one, not too far away, heads turned towards them, ears pricked, eyes shining.

'Oh yes,' she sighed.

'You called them, Sylvia.'

'As if! They were there, anyway, weren't they?'

'Were they?'

They watched the deer turn away from them, disappear among the trees.

'Lovely things!' she whispered.

'Yes. Very shy. Very strange. Very wild.'

He smiled.

'Very Sylvia,' he said.

They wandered on through the dark forest.

Time passed.

'What about school?' she asked.

'Ha! School! I don't go. Not now. Mebbe one day

I'll go back again.'

They wandered on.

'The brain again,' he said.

She waited.

They wandered on.

'I'm very clever,' he continued.

'Oh, aye?'

'I'm not showing off. It's just true. They talked about my amazing brain, ever since I was a kid. Oh Gabriel, you're amazing! What a clever boy you are!'

'Lucky you.'

'Think so? They made me do my GCSEs early. I passed them all. They wanted to make me go into the sixth form early and I was on my way. Then I started to see that I didn't want to be clever Gabriel. And I looked at the sixth form. They wanted me to wear a *suit*. I couldn't do it. So I left.'

'Because of a *suit*?'

'The suit and everything else. They told me a boy like me could do anything, be anything. My brain was a thing to pass all the exams with, a thing to think the same old thoughts with, a thing to go to Oxford with so they could look at me and say look how clever that Gabriel is, look how bloody accomplished he is! We have the highest expectations of him. The world's his bloody oyster! He'll be successful and rich. He'll be banker! A lawyer! A politician! A . . . High expectations. Jesus, how pathetic.'

'What do you want to be?'

'I don't know. A thing that does more than think. A thing that does more than keep things the way they've always been. A thing that can play the hollow bone! Hahaha!'

He went on laughing bitterly as he hurried on, then he stopped. He pulled back the sleeve of his right arm.

She saw the scars, the curves where the razor or the knife had cut into his tender skin.

He pulled back the sleeve on his other arm.

There were scars there too.

Tears came to his eyes.

He slid the sleeves back down.

'Sorry,' he said. 'Don't want to scare you. Shouldn't have shown you.'

'It's OK, Gabriel.'

She gently touched his arm.

'It's not just me, is it?' he said.

She thought of the children her mum worked with,

the sad tales she'd been told about them. She thought of kids in her own school.

'I know kids who have done the same,' she said.

He nodded.

They walked on.

The track sloped upwards now. They came to another clearing. There was a section of rock art there: curves and spirals and whirls on a hump of black rock. They crouched before it on the turf and ran their fingers across it. Sylvia closed her eyes. Inside herself, she slipped away from Gabriel. She tried to become the young woman who had crouched here in the distant past to create these shapes. How had the world been then? Did the skylarks sing? Did the deer come, called by the hollow bone? Did young people wander together across the earth, talking with each other, sharing silences with each other? Did young people harm themselves, like Gabriel? Did they ache with the delight and pain of being young?

'Was it painful?' Sylvia said softly.

'Aye.'

He raised his left sleeve again, traced the scars

with the tip of his finger.

She asked if she could touch and he said yes of course.

So she touched, gently, and he smiled, then lowered the sleeve again.

'Madness,' he said. 'But the wrong kind of madness.'

They sat beside the rock.

'They wanted me to go to hospital,' he said after a time. 'They said it would just be for a little while for checks and assessments and to give me time for myself. I went to see. They were very nice, very kind. I think I was very ill, and I was ready to go along with it, but in the end . . .'

She asked nothing.

'And then dad said, how about if we all go away, leave all this behind for a while?'

'And so you ended up here?'

'Aye. And I'm better than I've ever been,' he said.

'I'm pleased, Gabriel,' she said.

They drank some water. Gabriel had some chocolate which they shared.

'I've told nobody else these things,' he said.

'Thank you.'

They sat on the rock in silence.

They let the light fall on them. They listened to the silence which was not silence but was filled with the sound of breeze in the trees, of birdsong, of rustlings, of their own breathing and heartbeat.

Sylvia lay down on the soft turf beside the rock. An ant crawled across the skin of her arm. A tiny spider moved across her hand. Flies buzzed around her head.

A patch of daisies was growing at her side. Gabriel picked some and started to make a daisy necklace.

She closed her eyes. If she lay still for a long time, she wondered, how much life would gather on her? Would she be like a natural part of the forest floor? Would she merge with the earth beneath her? Would plants grow on her? Would beasts burrow through her? Would she blend with the rest of creation?

She breathed, breathed.

Time passed. The sun passed slowly through the sky.

'I could just lie here forever more,' she sighed.

'Me, too. But we'd be pretty cold tonight.'

She smiled and sat up.

It was like coming up from a dream, up from sleep.

'Guess we'd better get on,' he said.

'Where to?'

'Wherever we're going.'

He laughed.

'We'll know it when we get there, I guess,' he said.

He reached down and she took his hand and he helped her up.

He gave her the daisy necklace. She put it around her neck. She felt the flowers against her skin, loved the feeling of the flowers against her skin.

'Beautiful,' he said.

'Lead on, Gabriel,' she said.

They wandered on between the trees.

They came to a gap and Gabriel pointed to the lake a few miles away.

'Dive down into that and you'll find a village. You'll find a railway line and a school. They built a dam. They flooded the valley and the village and now you'd never guess there'd been people there at all.'

Their shoulders touched.

'Maybe that's how everything'll be in the end,' he said. 'No humans at all. Maybe that'd be for the best.'

He pointed to the crows above the trees. He talked about the squirrels and the deer.

'They'd be better off without us, wouldn't they?'

'Don't you think we're worth saving?' she said.

'Maybe if we change. If we stop screwing up everything.'

'If we rewild ourselves?'

'Something like that.'

They walked through the scents of the trees and the undergrowth, the singing of birds. She crouched and spread her hands across the earth. It was cold and soft and damp against her skin. She pressed her palms against the bark. She rubbed her hands across her cheeks. She felt the grains of earth, the coolness of water on her skin.

She felt the closeness of the trees to herself, of the earth to herself, of the air to herself. She was not just Sylvia. She was these things too. They were her. She was the forest, she was the earth, she was the air. They gave each other life. She wanted to love them and they wanted to love her. Why did we not realise that when we do things to the earth, we do things to ourselves; when we harm the earth, we harm ourselves?

It was like a veil had fallen from her eyes.

She was seeing beauty like she'd never seen it before.

It was like a veil had fallen from her mind.

She was thinking thoughts she'd never thought before.

'We're so stupid,' she murmured.

'Maybe our stupidity is a kind of cleverness,' she said.

She tried to turn her thoughts to words.

'We love the earth,' she said. 'In the deepest depths of ourselves, we know we love the earth. We're not just here, *on* it. We *are* it. It is us. And we are in love.'

'Tell that to the burners and polluters,' he said. 'Tell that to the bomb makers.'

'Even them. They've been spoiled and stunted. They've grown up all wrong. Maybe they burn because of their own distress. Maybe they bomb because they're in despair.'

They wandered on. She didn't want to think these thoughts but they kept on coming to her.

'And maybe they act on our behalf,' she said.

He said nothing.

'Because deep inside ourselves, we know that, for the sake of the world, we need to be finished off.'

'So we're killing ourselves for the sake of the world?'

'Yes!'

She rushed on now, letting the awful thoughts be released into awful words.

'And we do it faster and faster. We bomb and bomb. We let the world heat up fast so that we won't be able to survive in it. We know it's got to be finished fast, we know we have to get it all over with, to get it done quick, so that everything that's left can start to recover.'

'So we're committing suicide?' he said.

She pondered.

'No! Not suicide. Sacrifice. We're sacrificing ourselves for the sake of the world. We're destroying ourselves so that the world can be recreated once we're gone.'

'Hell's teeth,' said Gabriel.

'Hell's teeth,' Sylvia replied.

And another thought leapt suddenly to her mind. It brought her to a halt. She looked at him.

'Did *you* think of it?' she said. 'Did *you* want to commit suicide?'

'Yes.'

He said it quickly, then looked away from her.

'Yes,' he said again. 'There were moments when it seemed the only thing to do. There were moments when it seemed the *best* thing to do. The world would be better off without me.'

'Oh, Gabriel.'

He looked at her again.

'I know,' he said. 'Oh, Gabriel. Poor boy. But I'm OK now. I really am, Sylvia. Getting stronger. Getting braver.'

He moved on quickly through the forest. She walked at his side.

She wanted all the awful thoughts to be gone from her, all the thoughts about Gabriel and about destruction, but they wouldn't be gone from her.

They came to another small clearing where they let time pass, and where they ate some food.

She thought of a world without Gabriel in it, without any humans in it.

'Who would look at the rock art?' she said. 'Who would look at the deer and the trees? Who would blow through the hollow bones?'

How strange it seemed to her, that the world might go on existing, but that there might be no humans to be in it, no humans to experience it, no humans simply to look at it.

They walked on and she looked as she walked. How beautiful it all was, how very ordinary and very miraculous. She reached out and touched bark and leaves. She opened her ears and heard the singing of birds, the sighing of breeze, the swish of their feet. She opened her eyes wide to the dappled light. Her mind reeled. The beauty of the world poured into her. How could there be such light, such colour, such beauty? How could the world be so physical, so present, so real, and so filled with mystery? How could we cause such damage to this place? How could we think of leaving it?

'Oh, Gabriel,' she sighed. 'Just look how beautiful it all is.'

'I think that's what made me strong. I think that's what saved me. Just that. Just the beauty of the world.'

'Yes!'

'How could I think of leaving it? How could *anybody* think of leaving it?'

'Maybe a few of us will be left,' she said, 'to start again, and to do it better this time.'

'Or make the same mistakes again.'

'Maybe we don't have to.'

'Maybe to be human is to make the same mistakes.'

'Maybe there's other humans, somewhere out there in the universe, who haven't made the same mistakes.'

'So would they be human?'

'What does it mean, to be human?'

They walked on, fascinated and troubled by their thoughts that roamed from grains of earth to the stars of distant galaxies.

They wandered through themselves as well as through the forest.

They wandered through time. Moment by moment by moment, they walked through the present. Moment by moment, they stepped into the future. Moment by moment, they moved back into the past.

Sometimes their arms and shoulders brushed against each other. Who was this? She had never known anyone like him. What was it that drew her towards him, that caused her to walk so freely with him, to think such thoughts with him? Where was this leading her?

She turned her thoughts away from suicide and sacrifice. She turned them to this boy at her side, to her friends at home, to Maxine and Mickey and Francesca, to the friends she danced with, to the community she stood among at the Monument.

'It doesn't need to end in destruction,' she said.

'We are better than that,' she said.

'We can change all that,' she said.

'Who can?' asked Gabriel.

'We can. We are the ones who can change the world. We, the weird, passionate, troubled, loving young.'

On they wandered, on and on.

Sylvia wanted to find another clearing where they could sit close together on an ancient rock to talk, to seek the roots and seeds of hope.

But they found something else instead. They stopped, dead still.

There it was, dangling above them in the branches of a tree.

'Buzzard,' Gabriel whispered.

Its wings were spread wide, as if it had tried to fly free of its final agony.

Gabriel took off his rucksack. He climbed towards it.

Very gently, he disentangled it. He leaned down and held out the bird to her. She reached up and took it from him in both hands.

Very gently, she lowered it to the ground.

Its wings were as wide as her outstretched arms.

A lethal thing of feathers and beak and claws, of

strength and grace and tenderness.

The bird was half-decayed, all dried out.

They saw the wound in the bird's breast, the opening.
Gunshot wound.

'They say they go looking for rabbits or ducks or rats,' said Gabriel, 'but they can't help themselves. They see a thing of beauty – something more beautiful than they'll ever be – and they can't stand it. They've got to destroy it.'

She spread her hands wide upon it, felt the miracle of feathers and bone and flesh against her skin.

So beautiful, so savage, so sacred.

Her tears fell: to encounter so intimately the careless cruelty of humankind.

'We should bury it,' she said.

'No need,' he answered. 'It'll decay and become part of the earth. It'll be eaten and become part of everything. Look. The maggots are at it. The insects are feeding.'

She saw the maggots, the insects.

'The buzzard dies,' she said, 'and in its death, it helps give life.'

'Destruction and creation,' said Gabriel. 'Hand-in-hand. All at once.'

She stroked the softness of the feathers, touched the flinty sharpness of the claws and beak. She rested her two hands on the creature, so beautiful even in its death.

'Maybe it's been waiting here for you, Sylvia,' said Gabriel.

'Maybe this is where your hollow bone is found,' he said.

She didn't understand, but she also thought that somehow she did understand.

'We have to thank the buzzard for its life,' he said. 'We have to apologise for what brought it to its death.'

They knelt on the earth. She closed her eyes and whispered her thanks. When she was little, they made her say prayers at school, to a god that she never believed in, even then. The words were always meaningless to her. But the words of thanks and praise she murmured now to a creature of the earth and sky did feel like a true prayer.

When she silently apologised, the apology was to the whole of creation.

'Forgive us all,' she whispered.

'I should have brought a knife,' said Gabriel.

Sylvia wiped away her tears, then opened her rucksack.

'It's OK,' she said. 'I came prepared.'

She took out the knife.

'We need the wing,' he said.

She peered at him.

'That's where the hollow bone will be,' he said.

So she started to cut away the wing.

Back through the forest with the wing in her hand. It was almost as long as her arm, as broad as her chest.

So light for its size, it felt like a thing made almost of air.

They walked quietly, back through the dead straight trees, back through the clearings, back past the rock art, the shining pool. Flies buzzed around the thing. She had to keep wafting them away. Tiny creatures crawled from it on to her fingers. She brushed them gently away with her free hand.

At the forest's edge, they paused.

So strange to see open space, the stream, the bridge, the fallen totem poles, the village.

It was late afternoon now. Not long till dusk.

The sun was falling to the west.

'How will we do it?' said Sylvia.

'I'll put it in my dad's shed,' said Gabriel. 'We can work on it tomorrow.'

They carried the wing to Gabriel's garden.

They laid it on a bench in his father's shed.

They closed the shed again.

It was as if she had been stunned, but now she saw the garden.

Many vegetables were growing there.

There was a greenhouse.

There was a small wind turbine, its blades spinning fast in the breeze.

'Dad'll be picking Colin up,' he said. 'He'll be back soon.'

They stood as if they didn't know what else to say to each other, how to be with each other now.

'I'll tell him how the wing got there,' he said, 'if he asks.'

She was silent, suddenly again so shy, so shy.

This was all so new, this boy, this bird, this place.

'I'll go,' she murmured.

But she paused.

She breathed. She felt so different from how she

had felt just this morning. New thoughts, new sensations, new movements in her mind and her body. This new boy.

She murmured the words again, and didn't move again.

They gazed at each other.

The falling golden sun was shining in his eyes. It was glowing in his hair.

She wanted to say to him, 'You are very beautiful, Gabriel.'

She wanted him to say to her, 'You are very beautiful, Sylvia.'

The birds of dusk sang all around them.

She glimpsed a deer, moving just beyond the limits of the garden.

'We'll meet again,' she murmured. 'Tomorrow.'

'Aye. Tomorrow, Sylvia.'

'Aye.'

They tore themselves away.

Back home, she couldn't keep still. Her mum wanted to talk about the day.

'Yes,' Sylvia said. 'I had a good time, Mum.'

'You like him, then?'

Sylvia blushed.

'Yes, Mum. We walked through the forest.'

Her mother smiled.

'We just wandered,' said Sylvia. 'We saw some deer and some squirrels. And some rock art.'

How could she say her mind was a forest? How could she say she cut the wing off a buzzard, that she was going to make a flute from it? She hardly even knew what she was doing or why she was doing it herself.

'We saw some totem poles,' she said. 'We saw a baby starting to walk.'

'Did he talk about himself?'

'A bit.'

'It seems they've given up everything for a while. His dad was a carpenter. They're having a kind of family gap year.'

Sylvia was hardly listening. She could feel the weight of the wing in her hand. She wanted to move on, to get the knife in her hand again, to start cutting again.

'He brought the boys up on his own,' she said. 'The mother died soon after Colin was born.'

Sylvia gasped.

'He didn't tell me. Poor Gabriel.'

'Poor all of them.'

'How do you know?'

'I had coffee with him.'

'Oh. Right.'

'I did some sketches of him. See?'

She held up some pencil sketches. Anthony, sitting in an armchair. Anthony in profile. Anthony, full face.

'They're very good, Mum.'

'He's a nice man.'

'That's good.'

Her mum put the sketches down and laughed.

'Where are you, Sylvia?'

Sylvia blinked.

'Sorry. No news, I suppose?'

'About Dad? No. There will be soon. He'll be OK.'

'Photographing horrors.'

'Aye. Photographing horrors.'

They sat and read beneath two reading lamps. Sylvia couldn't read. The words were black marks on a bright white page with no meaning to them.

She felt the weight of the wing in her hand. She felt

her feet stepping across the forest floor. She felt Gabriel walking at her side. She saw his face, his eyes, the marks on his skin. She heard his voice.

'You OK, love?' said her mother.

'Aye, Mum.'

She wanted to say,

This place is doing something weird to me, Mum.

But how could she explain what she meant by those words?

Maybe this place was bringing out the weirdness that had always been in her. Maybe it brought out a weirdness that was in everybody.

She was restless, jumpy.

The light had gone outside.

'Think I'll go out,' she said suddenly.

'Out? Where to? To see Gabriel?'

'No. Up on to the fell and see the stars.'

Her mum laughed.

'Don't get lost.'

'I can't get lost.'

Up through the starlit path to the fell, to the stars.

She called Maxine.

'I can see you, Maxine!' she said when her friend answered.

'Oh aye?'

'Yes, I can. I can see the lights of the city glowing in the dark.'

'Are you drunk?'

'Oh, Maxine, The signal's so strong tonight! I'm out on the fell in the pitch-black night. But it isn't pitch-black night at all. The stars, Maxine! The bliddy galaxies! They're dancing! It's like I could just reach up and almost touch them. And there you are, a gentle glowing far off in the south. I'm waving, Maxine! Wave back to me.'

'I'm waving, Sylvia. Yoohoo! How was it today?'

'Today?'

'With *him*, you nit!'

The signal faded.

Crackle crackle fade fade.

She waved her phone, her wand.

The stars so abundant, scattered thickly across the endless sky. So bright, so clear. Stars between stars, stars beyond stars. How was there any dark at all? She stood on tiptoe, reached for them, and yes, she could almost touch, could almost gather a handful of them for herself. She opened her mouth wide and breathed in deep, felt she could breathe a galaxy down into herself.

Come into me, stars. Enter me, galaxies. Soar down deep into me, comets and meteors and . . .

'Hello?'

'Oh Maxine, it is so beautiful! If only you could—'

'So what did you *do*? What did he . . .'

Crackle crackle. Fade fade. Wave wave.

'Maybe I'm the feral child my dad said I am. Maybe I'm truly a child of the forest. Maybe I'm a child of the night . . .'

'Maybe what and maybe *what*?'

Crackle crackle. Fade fade. Wave wave.

'There *must* be others, Maxine.'

'Must be *what*?'

'Others out there in the universe, waiting for our call. Others calling to us. They listen for them, you know. Aliens. Every day and every night we scan the skies, searching for their signal.'

'. . . just going daft . . .'

'Hahaha! Maybe, yes! And they might not be there at all. And they might have been there once but not any more. But yes, they might.'

'*Tell* me, Sylvia!'

'It's *so* amazing. No such thing as darkness here. No such thing as silence.'

'. . . as *what*?'

'And maybe I can find the way to be myself out here. And maybe I can find the way to change the world out here.'

Crackle crackle. Fade fade.

'You're in *love*!'

'Eh?'

'Aye. With *Gabriel*!'

'Hahahah! With *everything*, Maxine!'

'. . . or bonkers, then . . .'

'Aye, bonkers then. Crackpot Sylvia on the fell in the night . . . Wave to me, Maxine?'

'What?'

'Wave, wave. Can you see me? Here I am, far out here in the night. I'm looking towards Newcastle. I can see the sky glowing over it. I can see you! Hello, Maxine!'

'Hahahaha! Hello, Sylvia, you crazy lass!'

'Are you waving?'

Crackle crackle. Fade fade.

'What?'

'Waving?'

'Yes! Yoohoo! Yoohoo!'

'Yoohoo!'

'Night night, you lovely nut!'

'Night night.'

And switch it off. And silence.

And those stars and those galaxies, and that weird carved rock beneath her feet. And oh this air and oh that owl and oh those scratchings and oh her beating heart.

And oh to be Sylvia out on the fell in the pitch-black night, to know trouble and pain, to know murdered beasts and damaged earth, and despite it all to ache with weird joy.

And hear the sudden cry of life that leaps from her.

The dead thing seethed with life. There were worms in the wing. Maggots squirmed in the flesh. Bugs crawled through the feathers. There was wetness and slime and such a stench.

They set a massive metal pot of water to boil above a massive fire.

Sylvia lifted the wing and plunged it in.

She held it in place in the water with a stick.

One minute, two minutes, three minutes, four.

She lifted it out again.

She shook it. Dead worms and maggots and bugs dropped out.

They set to, detaching the feathers from the flesh, tugging and twisting with fingers and thumbs. Sylvia cut and scraped with her scraper and knife.

Out came the feathers, such lovely things.

They laid them in order on the table to dry.

They were in Gabriel's garden.

They sat on old wooden chairs at an old wooden table on the grass.

Gabriel hummed some old song from the music night.

Gabriel's father came out.

Sylvia hadn't met him yet.

'This is Sylvia,' said Gabriel.

'Aye, I guessed as much.'

He held out his hand and she was about to take it when he laughed and suddenly withdrew it again.

He laughed.

'I've just seen where that hand's been,' he said. 'Sorry. But nice to meet you, Sylvia. I see he's got you involved in a project. Where's this come from?'

Gabriel told him the tale of the bird. His father grunted.

'There's always them that like to slaughter. So what you doing with it now?'

Gabriel shrugged.

'Just getting down to the bones, Dad,' he said.

His father nodded, as if this was a perfectly normal thing to do.

He was a big man. Jeans and an ancient blue shirt. Blue eyes and blond hair like his boys. He looked kindly upon Sylvia.

'It's good to have you here,' he said. 'I'm Anthony.'

He lifted a feather, a long flight feather, murmured his appreciation.

'Could anything be made more beautiful than this?' he said.

Sylvia shook her head.

'It couldn't,' she said.

'You'll be good for him,' he said. He gently cuffed his son's shoulder. 'But don't let him take you wandering to places you don't want to go.'

He went away. They went on with their work. More of the great flight feathers. The smaller, more tender ones. Then the tiny inner ones, so soft, so delicate.

They tugged them all away.

There the wing lay, featherless, the flesh close to the bone part-rotted, part-cooked. A few last worms somehow still survived in it.

Sylvia took the scraper in her right hand, held down the wing with her left, and started to scrape the flesh away.

All her senses were alert. She became lost in the task.

Gabriel hummed his tune.

In her mind, Sylvia heard the buzzard's cry in the song of her friend.

Flesh came away quite easily.

She got through to the bone.

Shreds of flesh remained.

She plunged the wing into boiling water again.

She pressed down on it with her stick to hold it there.

One minute, two minutes, three minutes, four.

Last fragments of flesh fell away, seethed with the water above the flame.

She lifted out the wing again. Scraped again. The wing was now a set of linked bones, hot and steaming, pale and bleached.

They laid it on the table next to the feathers to let it dry.

'The wing is an arm,' said Gabriel. 'It's just like ours. It has an upper arm like ours, and the bone like ours is called the humerus. It has a lower arm and ...'

She gasped. Second year biology with Mr Atkinson! She reached down to touch.

'That's the radius,' she said. 'That's the ulna.' She gripped her own arm, felt through the skin and the flesh to what lay beneath. 'The bones of the buzzard are just like the bones in us.'

'But they're hollow,' said Gabriel, 'so that the bird is light enough to fly.'

'Yes.'

She touched the bones again.

She thought of them beating, raising a body from earth.

She spread her arms wide and laughed as she imagined feathers on them.

Birdy Sylvia.

Buzzard Sylvia.

'Each bone a hollow bone,' she said. 'Each bone a musical instrument.'

'The whole bird a musical instrument,' said Gabriel.

'That's so beautiful!' they said together.

They laughed into each other's eyes.

She breathed. She contemplated. Which bone would be best?

'The ulna,' she said. 'That's the one.'

It was longer than the humerus, as long as the radius, broader than it.

She took the knife in her hand. Tried to saw the ulna, close to the elbow joint. It was difficult. Stone on bone. Her movements felt awkward. The stone slipped. It might break the bone rather than cut cleanly through it. She paused. She didn't want to ruin this. Didn't want to fail. Didn't want the buzzard to have given up its wing in vain.

'I'll get something else,' said Gabriel.

He went into the shed and came back with a little hacksaw. It was almost brand-new. Narrow blade, tiny sharp steel teeth.

She took it from him.

She sawed, slowly, carefully.

It would cut through easily, but straightaway she knew it wasn't right.

She put it down and took up the ancient knife again.

'We have to do it right,' she whispered. 'Have to do it in the proper way.'

She closed her eyes. Breathed deeply. Felt the knife balanced perfectly in her hand. Tried to feel as a girl from six thousand years ago might feel as she made her hollow bone.

She began again to saw the ulna, close to the elbow joint.

Moved her hand back and forth, moved the stone knife back and forward across the surface of the bone.

Did not press hard, remained calm, breathed slowly, let the stone edge cut at its own speed.

Yes. It worked. The stone slowly cut right through the bone.

She meditated again, breathed, relaxed, and started to cut again, this time close to the wrist joint.

Yes. It worked.

She lifted the ulna away from the other bones.

It was longer than her hand, just broader than her thumb. An elegant curve to it.

So strong, so frail.

She raised it to the sky, peered into it, saw the light pouring through the hollow bone.

She sighed.

What was this strange feeling, or this sudden loss of feeling? She seemed to stop being Sylvia, seemed to stop being anything at all. She shook her head, called herself back into herself.

She plunged the bone into the water again to boil infection away.

Lifted it out.

Laid it down on the table to cool and dry.

'We're mad,' she murmured.

'Yes,' said Gabriel.

She raised it to her lips and blew. No note of course came out.

They inspected Gabriel's own hollow bone, saw how the mouthpiece had been smoothed and rounded. She recalled the recorder from her childhood.

Gabriel brought a metal file.

She shook her head.

She found a flat stone on the ground. She used it as a file, slowly smoothing one end of the bone, creating the curve.

She blew again. Breath flowed through more easily now. But still no note.

'Needs a fingerhole,' she said.

She gripped the knife in her palm, meditated,

breathed, pressed the pointed end against the bone, twisted gently, gently, was wary again of cracking open the whole thing. But her hands and fingers and mind worked together, as if somehow she if she knew exactly what to do.

The stone bit into the bone.

She twisted.

Further into the bone.

A hole was formed. She widened it with the point, smoothed the edges of the hole with the scraper then with the stone.

Plunged the bone into the boiling water again.

Disappeared from herself again as she pressed the bone down into the water with the stick.

Took it out again.

Let it cool.

Lifted it to her lips and blew again.

Nothing, just the sound of breath.

Looked closely at it, remembered the recorder, looked at Gabriel's hollow bone. She thought of tin whistles, clarinets, oboes.

'The mouthpiece should be narrower,' she whispered. 'So that the breath's concentrated and then released.'

'Like when you whistle,' he said.

He shaped his lips, he whistled.

They both smiled.

A bird was singing in a tree nearby, notes pouring from its throat, its beak.

They pondered.

Fallen twigs lay under the tree.

She picked one up and inspected it.

No good.

Another. Another.

She peeled the bark away from one of them. She cut a short section with the knife, a centimetre or so long.

Started to carve and shape it with the scraper and the stone so that it might fit into the opening of the bone. She tried it, carved again, smoothed again. She shaped it so that when she pushed it into the opening of the bone, the opening would be narrower than the rest.

She pressed, wedged it there. It wouldn't stay.

'Needs glue,' said Gabriel.

'Not glue. Something older.'

They pondered.

'Egg,' he muttered.

He went into the house, came out with an egg in a bowl. Cracked the egg into the bowl. As if she knew exactly what to do, she dipped her finger into the albumen. Smeared a little on to the fragment of wood. She slipped the wood into the opening again and held it there.

It didn't shift.

They waited as it set.

'Don't teach you this in school, do they?' he said.

'As if,' murmured Sylvia.

She held the bone gently on her palms.

Then lifted it to her lips and blew.

Too hard.

She breathed more gently.

More of a squeak than a proper note, but yes, there was the frail beginning of a note.

She adjusted her breathing, gained some control.

There was a note, the beginning of music.

She breathed gently. The note was hardly audible.

She opened and closed the fingerhole as she blew. The note shifted, changed.

She used the knife again to form another fingerhole.

Smoothed it with scraper and stone.

She blew again. Moved her fingers on to and off the fingerholes.

The notes changed.

She laughed.

Gained in confidence.

Yes, she was beginning to understand how to do this thing.

She held in her hands a fragile flute

formed of a bone from a buzzard's wing,

a flute that was like the first of all flutes.

She blew through a hollow bone.

Frail music was drawn from deep inside herself.

It moved through her

and through the bone of the bird

and it became stronger

and was concentrated then released

into the empty air around herself and Gabriel.

It flowed into the air of the garden

and the air of Northumberland

and into the high wide Northumbrian sky.

Sylvia shifted her feet as if in a dance.

Sylvia was Sylvia and not Sylvia.

She was the music.

She was the hollow bone.

She danced with Gabriel.

They danced to the first music in Gabriel's garden,

while a bird sang above them in the tree.

The girl came that night.

There was no sound to her.

But there was a scent, a smell.

A smell of brackish earth, of woodsmoke and sweat.

Maybe it was this that woke Sylvia.

She opened her eyes, turned in her bed.

The girl was by the window. Beyond her were the stars.

The girl's hair was long, flaxen. She wore some kind of shift, of wool or animal skin. She was as tall as Sylvia. When she turned, her face was pale. Dark eyes, dark mouth. A necklace dangled from her. Some kind of bracelet on each wrist.

Her gaze rested on Sylvia for a moment.

There was no fear.

Neither girl recoiled.

The girl reached down to the table by Sylvia's bed. She lifted the scraper and held it in her hand. It fitted easily between her fingers. She held it before her eyes, then moved it, as if scraping something that only she could see. She lifted the knife and cut something that only she could see. She was relaxed. She placed the

119

scraper and the knife back on to the table.

She lifted the hollow bone, held it before her eyes, turned it carefully in her fingers, rested it on her palms.

Her shoulders relaxed, as if she were sighing.

As she raised it to her lips, she gazed again upon Sylvia.

She played the hollow bone.

There was no music to be heard.

Just silence as her fingers rose and fell upon the fingerholes, as her cheeks and lips moved upon her silent breath.

There was nothing at all to be heard.

No sounds from the night.

No sounds from Sylvia herself.

It was as if the silence had absorbed all sound.

It was as if the silence *was* all sound.

The girl played for a while, then took the instrument away from her lips. With her two hands, she placed it back upon Sylvia's table.

There was a single click as the bone returned to the table.

The girls looked at each other.

The girl crouched and reached down to the floor.

There was a fragile scraping as she moved her index finger across the floor.

The girl stood again.

In her last lingering look there was the beginning of a smile.

And she was gone.

Just the window, the night, the stars.

Sylvia slept.

Next morning, soon after dawn, she crouched where the girl had crouched.

There were traces of finger marks there.

Sylvia followed them with her own index finger.

She heard the music in those shapes.

She felt the curves and spirals of them in her mind.

Next day, Sylvia pulled on her walking boots and waterproofs, and went high on to the fell alone.

She took no phone with her.

She stood on the rock art and played the hollow bone.

She learned how to play by playing it.

Finches sang nearby. Birds of prey wheeled high above.

On another fell, a family of deer moved through the

heather and bracken. They paused to gaze at her, to listen, then wandered on, relaxed, at ease, at home.

A fox moved across the pathway higher up. It too paused to look down at her, to listen. The redness of its coat, the glitter of its eye. It watched for moments while she played and then moved on.

A familiar ache of loss and dread and longing came into her, but she went on playing and the ache of loss and dread and longing flowed with the music into the air.

The breeze played upon her.

The dampness in the air dampened her cheek.

A silent jet, far off.

She regarded it calmly and played on.

Her feet and her body were of the rock.

Her breath and her mind were of the air.

Her music made the rock and air as one.

She swayed, reeled.

She moved out of herself with the music.

She moved out of herself and looked upon herself and felt that she could walk away and keep on walking and there would still be a Sylvia Carr on the rock, playing, playing.

She felt like she could turn to a skylark and leap from

the earth into the air and look down and there would still be a Sylvia Carr on the rock, playing, playing.

The birds sang and called.

The air and the earth sang and called.

Oh, the beautiful loss of herself in the earth and the air and the music.

Oh, the . . .

'Sylvia! Sylvia Carr!'

She flinched.

She snapped back into herself.

'Sylviaaaaa!'

The voice was Colin's, from far away.

Here he came, a tiny figure on the pathway lower down, running, calling.

Her name swirled around her.

She lowered the hollow bone and waited.

Like coming out of a dream.

No, not a dream. Something stronger, deeper, much much stranger.

Where have you been? she whispered to herself. *What the hell is happening to you?*

The boy came closer.

She felt the vibration of his voice on the air, of his feet on the earth.

He paused before he got to her.

'She didn't know where you were!' he said.

'She's been calling you!' he said.

What was he talking about?

She couldn't speak.

'Your mum!' he said.

The words seemed meaningless.

'She wants you to come!' he said.

She stepped from the rock.

She put the hollow bone into the pocket of the waterproof.

'Come on!' he said.

He turned, as if to lead her.

'Why?' she managed to say.

'Something's happened, Sylvia. She needs you to come.'

He looked back at her.

'Are you all right, Sylvia?'

She blinked, she nodded.

'Yes,' she grunted.

'Good!'

She followed him.

And the earth and the universe reeled and swirled around her as he led her down.

Her mum was at the car. She was putting a suitcase into the car.

'Where have you been?' she snapped at her daughter.

Sylva waved her arm towards the emptiness.

'Just there. Up there.'

'Up where? I've been calling you and calling you. Did you not *hear*?'

Sylvia stood there.

'*Sylvia!*'

'Sylvia *what*?'

'Something's happened. I've got to get back.'

Sylvia squeezed her eyes, trying to focus on what was happening.

'What something?' she said. 'Is it Dad?'

'It's one of the kids.'

'The kids? You're on *holiday*, Mum.'

'He ran away from home.'

'Who did? And all kids want to run away from home.'

'Malcolm. He's only twelve. He's calling for me.'

'*What*?'

'She said he won't talk to anybody but me.'

'Who said?'

'His mum.'

'His mum's phoning you when you're on holiday?'

'He said he wanted to do away with himself, Sylvia.'

'So it's a doctor's job.'

'He's seen a doctor. He wants to see me.'

'Oh, Mum.'

'Do you want to come?'

'What? Me? Why?'

'So you're not up here alone.'

'How long you going to be?'

'I dunno. Just a day or so. He's got *nobody*, Sylvia.'

'His mum?'

'You should meet his mum, love.'

Sylvia sighed. Her mother, the martyr.

'You'll be OK, won't you?' said her mum.

'It's only fifty miles away,' said Sylvia. 'It's not like I'm in Outer . . .'

'And there's Gabriel's family, isn't there. I've told Anthony. And there's Andreas.'

'Yes, Mum. Everything will be fine. Go and see your troubled boy. We have to save the troubled boys, don't we?'

'Yes, we do. You won't be scared?'

'*Mum.*'

'OK, love. I know. I'm stupid. I'm too soft.'

'You're lovely, Mum.'

'Am I?'

Sylvia leaned forward and kissed her mum's cheek.

'Yes. You are. Drive carefully.'

'I will. You'll be OK?'

'Yes, Mum.'

'You won't be scared?'

'*Mum.*'

Her mum got into the car, closed the door, drove from the village. With Colin at her side, Sylvia watched the car climb the curving road away from the village. She watched until the car and her mother were out of sight.

'Do you know Malcolm?' said Colin.

'No.'

'We'll look after you,' he said.

'I don't need looking after.'

She fingered the hollow bone in her pocket.

There was silence all around.

She shuddered.

She felt a jolt of fear.

She went to the swings with Gabriel.

The chains rattled and creaked as they rocked back and forward, back and forward.

Neither of them said anything.

Gabriel hummed some folk tune to the rhythm of the swings.

'My mum told me about your mum,' she said.

'Oh?'

'I'm so sorry.'

'Sometimes I think I hardly remember her. Then I do. We talk about her. That keeps her with us.'

'That's good.'

'People never know what to say about it,' he said. 'Maybe there is nothing to say about it. She died. It was a long time ago.'

No, there was nothing to say.

They swung back and forward, back and forward.

'Bliddy death,' he said.

'Down with Death!' he yelled.

'Aye, Down with Death!'

A flock of starling screeched and scattered away.

They swung, they smiled, the chains creaked, their thoughts moved on.

'There was a girl,' said Sylvia.

'A girl?'

She just laughed. She couldn't go on. She couldn't tell him more. She just looked straight ahead, across the fells, into the sky.

'Yes,' she said, 'there was a girl, that's all.'

'Sounds like the beginning of a story. Or a song.'

He broke into song.

'There was a girl, that's all
And her name was Sylvia Carr
And she came to far Northumberland
And she met the strangest boy.'

He swung his legs and the swing rose higher and it creaked, creaked.

'And she found a bird
And she took its wing
And she took its bone
And went on a swing . . .'

He giggled.

'It is called,' he said, 'The Ballad of Sylvia Carr.'

He sang again.

'There's lots to sing about,' he said.

'Sing on,' she said.

'And she was small as a bird
And as strong as a bear,' he sang.

'*And as thing as a thing and as thing as another thing . . .*'

His song turned to laughter.

'Maybe your whole life is a ballad,' he said. 'Maybe everybody's life is a ballad. And if we get the words right and if we get the tune right, folk will go on singing it forever more!'

He sang,

'*La-la-la, little Sylvia Carr*

Lalalalala, great Sylvia Carr!'

And it all spiralled with their laughter out of the village, across the fells, into the boundless sky.

Back and forth, they went, up and down.

Rattle rattle. Creak creak.

Yes, I'm a story, thought Sylvia. *Yes, I'm a song.*

Back and forth, back and forth,

back and forth and up and down.

Rattle rattle. Creak creak.

'*Up with Life*,' sang Gabriel. '*And down down down with bliddy Death.*'

She ate that evening at Gabriel's house.

Anthony made a stew in a big black pot. A huge red garlicky thing with tomatoes and onions and beetroot and chickpeas. He splashed chilli into it as it bubbled on the stove. He roasted massive potatoes in the oven. The house was filled with delicious scents.

Colin set the table. He kept shifting his feet as if he were dancing to jagged music that only he could hear.

A fire blazed in the grate.

Sylvia sat in front of it on a sofa with Gabriel. He had a pen and a notebook. He wrote, crossed out, stared into space, closed his eyes, sighed, clicked his tongue, shook his head, scribbled again, laughed, sighed, wrote again, crossed out again, wrote again.

'I wish I was a bloody bird,' he said.

'A bird?'

'Aye. They don't have to write their songs, do they? They just open their beaks and out it pours.'

He pursed his lips. He whistled.

'Just like that!'

He laughed again.

'That sounds like a song as well,' he said. 'I Wish I Was a Bloody Bird.'

Sparks leapt from the fire. Sylvia quenched them with the soles of her boots.

Her mum called on the landline.

She'd been to see Malcolm. He was a lot calmer

now. He hadn't really wanted to do away with himself, of course. A cry for help, she said. She'd stay a while, just to help him get over it.

'I heard from your father too,' she said.

'From Dad? Where is he?'

'In bloody Rome, would you believe? Taking pictures of starlings and eating pasta and wanting to head back to Syria again.'

'To Syria?'

'The fool.'

'Oh, Mum.'

'He's as bad as Malcolm and the others. How you getting on?'

'Very well. Anthony's making stew.'

'How lovely. Can you put him on?'

'Anthony?'

'Yes. Just a quick word.'

She called Anthony and gave him the phone.

Anthony smiled as he talked.

'Yes,' he murmured. 'Yes, she's fine. It's nothing, Estella. You'd do the same for us.'

He laughed softly and said goodbye and gave the phone back to Sylvia.

Her mum's voice was softer, calmer.

'Maybe you should stay at Anthony's tonight,' she said.

'Maybe,' said Sylvia.

But she thought not. She'd be fine in the house on her own.

'Take it easy, Mum,' she said. 'Don't worry about Dad.'

'I will. I won't.'

'I love you, Mum.'

'I love you too. Sleep well, my little love.'

'I will. Sleep well.'

Back on the sofa, Gabriel wrote.

He paused and sung words under his breath.

She tried to hear and understand. She couldn't make them out.

He smiled at her.

'It'll come,' he murmured.

Then he went away and came back again. He had a photograph in his hand.

'This is her,' he said.

A dark-haired woman in jeans and a checked shirt, laughing and shielding her eyes against the sun.

'She looks lovely,' said Sylvia.

'She was. She is. Her name was Rebecca.'

'You look like her.'

'Yes. I do.'

He sighed.

'That's all,' he said.

He put the photograph away.

The sofa was comfortable, the fire was warm. He moved closer to her. Their hips and shoulders touched. They breathed easily.

He hummed a tune. Her mind drifted, drifted. The memory of the girl, the presence of the girl, was there, at the heart of everything.

'Grub's up!' said Anthony.

They went to the table.

Sylvia surprised herself. She ate hungrily, spooned two bowls of the red stew into herself. She ate two huge potatoes, as if she were preparing for some journey or some great exertion. She drank a little glass of white wine. They all ate some delicious lemon cake.

Anthony asked if she'd stay with them tonight.

She shook her head.

'Thank you,' she said. 'I'll be fine on my own.'

'If you're sure.'

'It's just along the street,' she said.

'You couldn't be in a safer place.'

She put on her waterproof and said good night.

Gabriel went out with her and walked with her.

They looked together at the rising moon.

They said that it was beautiful.

'*There was a girl*,' sang Gabriel softly, '*and her name was Sylvia Carr, and she met a rather weird boy and he said that she was beautiful.*'

'Did he?' she said.

He smiled, and the moon gleamed in his eyes.

'Aye, he did,' he said. 'He said that she was very beautiful.'

She sighed. She couldn't look at him.

Not now, she said inside herself.

They walked to her door.

'It's been an amazing day,' she said.

'It has.'

'Good night, Gabriel,' she said.

He sighed. A little note of disappointment.

'Good night, Sylvia,' he said. 'We're just along the street.'

'Good night.'

He walked away, his pale hair shining in the light of the moon.

She stepped all alone into the little dark house.

She went up to her bedroom, didn't undress.

She switched on a light. The curtains were open. The window was black rectangles with reflections of herself and the room in them.

She switched off the light and the reflections were gone.

She cupped her hands against the glass and stared.

There was the moon, there were the endless stars.

There was Newcastle, its distant dim glow in the south.

She imagined her mum at the heart of that glow.

Where was Rome? How far beyond?

How far south would she have to go

to see Rome aglow on the horizon?

And would he still be there, at the heart of that glow?

She sat on the edge of the bed,

at the heart of this Northern darkness

at the heart of this Northern silence.

She found herself wanting the girl to appear.

She knew that was why she'd come back alone.

She closed her eyes.

'Come now,' she whispered.

She opened her eyes again.

Nothing.

She played the hollow bone, gently, gently.

There was the sudden sound of someone laughing and the screech of an owl from outside.

'Come now. Please.'

Nothing, just the sound of laughter again, then silence.

She played the hollow bone. The music moved through the room and came back to her own ears.

Her own music was seeking her, calling her.

She whispered the words again, once, twice, three times, four.

The words left her lips and moved through the room.

And came back to her as she spoke them.

Come now, come now, come now, come now.

Her own words returned and whispered in her ear.

Her own words were seeking her, calling her.

Come now. Come now.

Sylvia, come now.

She clicked the front door shut, clicked the front gate shut.

She had on her walking boots, her waterproof.

She had the scraper, the knife, the hollow bone.

No lights in any of the houses.

Silence in the street, just the sound of her boots on the road.

She paused near Gabriel's house.

She heard his song.

There was a girl, that's all . . .

For a moment she imagined his arms around her, his lips upon hers. She'd been with boys before, but not with a boy like this boy. She turned her mind away. It wasn't time for that, she told herself. Not now. Maybe afterwards.

She frowned at herself: what did she mean by *afterwards*?

She walked on. She passed the club and the dilapidated telephone box and the dangling Christ. She came to the totem poles. The carvings in them were etched by the black shadows of the moon.

The world was silvery, shadowy.

She trembled as she crossed the stream. It ran fast below her, gurgling as it tumbled between its banks, over its bed of stone. She paused again. She hadn't planned to do this thing. She had just stepped out and started doing it. Was it possible that something really was guiding her, something was calling her?

Come now, Sylvia.

She came to the forest's edge, and paused. The straight track was before her, leading through the trees towards the depths. Shafts of moonlight fell through the trees. Patterns of moonlight lay on the floor.

Silly Sylvia, she whispered, for now she thought again of Snow White, Hansel and Gretel, Goldilocks. She thought of wolves and bears. She remembered weeping in fright as a child in Chopwell Wood when they went to buy the Christmas tree that year.

Silly Sylvia.

There were no dangers, she told herself. This wasn't Outer Mongolia. This was the tender north, a couple of hours' drive from her home. This was Northumberland.

She was Sylvia Carr, fifteen years old, an ordinary girl, a bold and shy and independent modern girl.

She raised the hollow bone and softly blew.

An owl came from behind her, a large pale thing beating its silent wings as it flew over her head and into the forest. It followed the straight track, moving from shadow to light, shadow to light. Sylvia watched it fade and disappear.

The forest was deep and still and beautiful.

It waited to welcome her.

Be brave, Sylvia, she told herself.

She played the hollow bone, gently, gently.

She took a breath and in she went.

And she had a sudden memory as the forest shadows fell upon her as she walked.

She was a little girl, in the kitchen at home in Newcastle. All three of them were there: Sylvia, her mum, her dad. She was nestled in the space between them on a sofa. She had a soft toy, a tiger called Belinda, on her lap. They were telling her, as parents do, of how she came to be.

Her mummy laughed.

'They looked *inside* me, Sylvia.'

'When I lived inside you, Mummy?'

'Yes, when you lived inside.' She rubbed her belly. 'Just here.'

They all put their hands there. Sylvia giggled.

140

'It must have been very, very dark in there!'

Her daddy laughed.

'Oh yes, it must have been. But a lovely nurse shone a kind of light in there and we all looked for you.'

'And did you see me?'

'They said you would be very tiny if we did.'

'As tiny as Belinda?'

'Oh much tinier than Belinda. As tiny as . . . a finger nail.'

'Or even tinier than that,' her mummy said. 'As tiny as a tiny beetle.'

Sylvia giggled. A beetle! Tiny beetle Sylvia.

'They said,' her daddy said, 'that when we did see you, we'd see you blinking.'

'Blinking?'

'Yes, blinking,' said her mummy. 'Like a bright star far far away in the sky.'

'Or like a tiny distant space ship,' said her daddy, 'heading down to earth.'

'And that would be your tiny, tiny beating heart,' her mummy said.

Sylvia gasped.

'And did you see?'

'Oh yes we saw,' her mummy said. 'We looked very

hard. And there you were, alive inside. Our little darling and her beating heart, our tiny beetle growing into a lovely girl.'

All three were silent, stunned by the enormity of such a thing.

They shuffled closer to each other. Sylvia held Belinda tight.

'Would it be scary in there?' said Sylvia.

'Oh no, my love,' her mummy said. 'Inside me was the safest place in all the world. We found you in the darkness and we knew that you would be born.'

'And look at you now,' her daddy said. 'Such a bonny blooming lass and getting bigger and bigger and stronger and stronger.'

They all laughed together.

'And I'll get bigger!' said Sylvia. 'I'll get big as a . . . horse. As big as a . . . house.'

'As big as a *house*?' her daddy said.

'Yes. And then Mummy and Daddy and Belinda can come and live inside *me*!'

'Excellent idea!' her mummy said.

'And *that* will be the safest place in all the world!'

Sylvia sighed as she walked, as such memories of infancy moved through her. And the shadows fell on her. And bats flickered through the moonbeams. And an owl screeched somewhere. And there were shufflings in the undergrowth. And a bark and a distant howl. And the dull drone of a distant aeroplane. And her feet moving on the earth. And her breath, in and out and in and out. And the memories of the closeness of her parents' bodies and their breath, of their voices whispering and comforting and praising, voices telling her of how splendid she was and how splendid she would always be. Sylvia Carr, growing into a girl, a young woman, bones and muscles growing stronger, mind expanding, shifting, learning. Sylvia Carr, moving freely through her city, stepping freely across the lovely earth. Sylvia Carr, with the song of life in her, with the song of all creation in her.

She raised the hollow bone and softly blew.

The sound was breath-like, bird-like.

The sound was very ancient, very new.

She blew gently. She heard rustlings nearby as the beasts came closer to her.

She lowered the hollow bone again and moved on again.

She heard Gabriel's voice, as if he were singing to her as she moved through the forest, as if the notes of his song were her footsteps, as if the tune was her journey. She moved forward to the rhythm of his song.

There was a girl, and her name was Sylvia Carr.

And then she felt the hand in hers.

It closed around her fingers, held her gently, tugged her gently.

Come now. Sylvia Carr.

Sylvia Carr, come now.

Deeper into the forest she went.

Who was with her? Maybe the girl. Maybe another. She could not see.

She shivered, but she wasn't afraid.

The hand was secure in hers, leading her on.

They stepped away from the track and moved through the gaps between the thick-trunked trees.

The earth was uneven. She brushed against the trunks. She ducked beneath the branches. She moved through shadow and moonlight. At one moment the hand that was guiding her gripped her more tightly. It held her back. They stood dead still. Something else was moving, not too far away. Sylvia heard its footsteps on the earth. She saw a great dark shifting form. She heard the snuffling of breath. It moved away. The hand relaxed. They moved on. The thought of turning back, of running back to the village, crossed Sylvia's mind. She let it pass. She must go on. She was Sylvia Carr. This was her story, this was her song. *Be brave*, she told herself. It was right that she should move like this through the forest, through the night. Something waited for her, not too far away. Something waited for her, once a little time had passed, once five thousand years had passed.

They moved on, moment by moment, step by step.

The earth became more even. The ground that had been gouged by the planting of the forest became softer, springier. The gaps between the tree trunks widened. The sky opened and there the full moon shone. They moved upwards now. They moved more quickly. The hand in hers was warm and strong.

They came to a hilltop. By the light of the moon, Sylvia saw the dark rock with the markings on it, the markings she had imagined on her own skin, that she had felt inside her own mind. The rock gleamed gently. And all around, the trees had changed. The tight-packed conifers were gone. The trees were in clusters, different shapes. Nearby a great tree spread its massive limbs across the sky.

And now the girl. Here she was, taking shape beside Sylvia. Hers was the hand in Sylvia's hand. She withdrew it now and stood there. Was she real? She was moonlit, like all the world. She was shadowed, like all the world. Again, the thought of turning back, of running, of rejecting what was happening, came to Sylvia's mind. Again, she turned from it.

Be still, she said inside herself. *Be brave*.

She breathed. She widened her mind and widened her eyes.

She did not resist.

She opened herself to what was happening to her.

She faced the girl, and the girl became more real as Sylvia looked at her, as the moon shone down at her. The girl allowed herself to be looked upon. She opened herself to what was happening to her. She was as tall as Sylvia. She was as old as Sylvia. Her face shone gently and her eyes gleamed. She wore a pale shift. She wore a necklace of what looked like seashells, bracelets of what looked like seashells. Her feet were bare.

She gazed directly back at the girl who gazed at her.

The girl stood relaxed and strong as Sylvia herself.

Sylvia looked upon her. Dressed differently, this girl could be one of her friends at school. She could be one of the kids at the Monument. She was very ancient, very new.

'My name is Sylvia,' said Sylvia.

The girl's face gently shifted, softened into a shadowed smile.

The scent of sweat and brackish earth and woodsmoke came again.

Now Sylvia heard the breathing of the girl.

She kept her eyes upon her.

'I am fifteen years old,' Sylvia said.

She groaned at herself. How could this girl understand such things?

'I am like you,' said Sylvia.

The girl gazed back.

'My name is Sylvia Carr,' said Sylvia.

'Who are you?' said Sylvia.

The girl took a stone knife from somewhere inside her clothing. She showed it to Sylvia. She crouched at the rock, and moved the point of her knife across it. She traced the shape of a spiral that connected with a spiral that was already there. She traced again, again, making a groove. She looked up at Sylvia. The moon shone in her eyes. Sylvia frowned, then understood. She took out her own knife from her waterproof, the one given to her by Andreas, the one that had cut her own skin. She took it out from its pouch. There were already markings on this rock, curves and whorls and spirals. Sylvia crouched beside the girl. With the point of her own knife, by the vivid light of the moon, she traced the shape of a spiral that connected with one that was already there. It was a spiral that was smaller than her own hand. She did not press hard. The stone of the knife was harder than the stone of the rock and the stone of the knife cut into the surface of the rock. The moonlight picked out the shadow of this new mark. She traced it again, pressing a little harder, making a groove like the girl's. The girl watched. Then she showed Sylvia a round stone that had been lying on the grass by the rock. She held this with her right hand. With her left hand, she held the blade of her knife in the groove. She tapped the back of the knife with the stone, using it like a hammer to push the knife forward, deepening the groove. She did this again, again. The spiral become deeper and clearer, more shadowed by the moonlight.

Sylvia understood. The girl handed her the hammer stone. It was a little bigger than Sylvia's fist. It fitted easily into her palm. She gripped it with her fingers. She held the knife blade in the groove. She gently tapped the back of the knife with the stone. The girl nodded. *That's right. That's right, Sylvia.*

The girl lifted another such stone from the grass.

The girls worked together, using their knives and hammer stones to create their art in the rock. They tapped, pushed and scraped. Again, again, again, again, their hands moved in spirals across the rock. Sylvia lost herself in the task, as she had when she cut into the bone of the bird. She was just her hand, the stone, the movement, the mark. She was in harmony with the girl beside her, who was also lost in the making of marks.

The two girls might have been there for hours, for years, as the spirals took shape beneath their hands.

They put the hammer stones aside, and they used the points of the knives again, spiralling, spiralling, smoothing the marks.

At last the girls leaned back. The shapes were done.

Now the girls made the curved marks that joined their spirals to each other.

They moved back from the rock again and looked down at it.

Sylvia smiled. The girl smiled.

There they were, brought together on the rock.

The girl put her knife away. Sylvia folded her knife into its pouch and put it away.

They laid their hammer stones on the grass.

And the girl reached out and took both of Sylvia's hands in her own.

And they stood up and held each other by the patterned rock and smiled into each other's eyes and they felt the strength and the tenderness in each other.

And Sylvia put her arms around the girl and the girl put her arms around Sylvia and they breathed against each other and they felt the beating of each other's heart.

And Sylvia Carr, this girl with such intensity of feeling, such intensity of thought, felt an intensity that she had never felt before, and as she and the girl released each other she stepped back and saw the flickering of firelight on the hillsides below her. She heard the laughter of children. She heard the voices of adults moving smoothly through the clear air. She saw moonlit figures moving across the earth. She saw the patterns of huts. It was like looking far into the deepest night, far into the unknown depths of her own mind.

And now the girl reached into Sylvia's waterproof and she took out the hollow bone and she lifted it to her lips and she looked into Sylvia's eyes and she played. She played for minutes that might have been a thousand years, and the music rose from her body and from the bone of the buzzard and from all the ages past and it travelled through the beautiful moonlit Northumbrian air, and through the body, mind and soul of Sylvia Carr.

And Sylvia became the music, and she could not move and could not speak and then at last she whispered to the girl.

'I am you.'

She laughed.

'And you are me,' she softly said.

And she looked back in the direction that she'd come from.

Everything was new, everything had changed.

How will I get back? she wondered to herself.

The girl touched Sylvia's cheek.

And Sylvia fell, and entered her dream.

She lay by the rock by the great tree with her arms outstretched, like the buzzard, the totem poles, the dangling Christ. The girl in the shift and the seashell necklace sat calmly in the moonlight at her side. Did Sylvia sleep, or did she die? Like the totem poles and the buzzard, she changed. She began to turn to earth. Her flesh and her bones decayed. Spiders and beetles crawled over her. Worms slid through her. Maggots fed on her. Moisture seeped up from the ground. Dew seeped down from the air. The earth took her to itself. Rain fell on her. Breezes blew across her. Winds came, and storms, and torrential rain and snow and sleet and frost and ice. There were times of bright sunshine and baking heat. And the earth turned and kept on turning and time passed and kept on passing. And the girl faded and other girls and other folk passed by and some lingered close to her. And lichen, flowers, moss and ferns grew on her. Bees buzzed over her. Adders crawled across her. Rabbits burrowed in her. Badgers dug down through her. Shrubs and trees grew from her and birds made nests in their branches and sang above her. And all these things fed on her and took nourishment from her and so she became these things. And bears and wolves and deer and foxes walked upon her. Children picked berries from the shrubs that grew upon her. A boy picked a linnet's egg from its nest just above her. A woman sat on the marked rock for many hours, weeping for her lost child. A couple lay upon her and loved each other and murmured that they would love each other always. And two men fought with knives and one man fell and crawled away with his lifeblood draining from him. And there was the clashing and wailing sounds of battles fought nearby. And in the silence afterwards came the calling of cuckoos and owls and skylarks, and the barking of dogs and the laughter of children. And the earth kept turning, turning, and time kept passing, passing. And sun rose and fell. Moon waxed and waned. Great galaxies wheeled and danced across the endless sky. And men came with implements and dug into the earth and a forest grew around her, a forest of straight trees with thick trunks and deep dark branches. And sometimes jets now screamed through the clear air above the trees. And one quiet sunlit crystal afternoon, a soaring buzzard mewed and there came a crack and the buzzard fell, beating its wings in the attempt to fly free of such pain. And it fell, and dangled in a tree close by her.

And here came a girl, and a boy, wandering together through the trees, talking of creation and destruction, to discover the feathered miracle wrought by all creation, to find a hollow bone that would make music to transcend time.

'Sylvia! Sylvia Carr!'

The piping voice was far, far away, young and bright in the early morning air.

'Sylviaaaaa!'

Did she hear it really, or was it in a dream?

Much closer were the voices of birds that rose from the forest and its clearings. Of robins and blackbirds, squawking crows, ravens and wrens and thrushes and finches. Over everything, skylarks sang and buzzards wheeled. The singing was drawn out from gorgeous hollow-boned bodies. It was forced through narrow throats and sharp wide-open beaks. It was the singing of air and earth and time. It signalled the end of night and welcomed the return of sun. Here it came, exposed again as the great world turned, great yellow ball of distant fire above the fells, above the trees, above the lake. The singing swirled out to it, spiralled in its light.

And it spiralled down to Sylvia Carr. It journeyed through her narrow ear, called through her growing body, poured into her wondrous mind, danced in her yearning soul.

And called her back from her sleep and from her death.

She opened her eyes.

The sky was crystal blue.

The earth was tender and warm.

She lay there waking.

Where was she? What was she? Was she being born?

Was this what the joy inside her was, the joy of being born?

She opened her mouth and let her own wordless song pour out from her.

It rose into the air and took its place among the chorus of the birds.

She felt her body, the bones, the flesh.

She tenderly touched the skin of her face.

She stroked her hair.

She looked down at herself.

She lay on the grass.

She wore her walking boots, her jeans, her waterproof.

She got up and knelt before the rock. There was white lichen growing there. Bright green moss grew in the grooves of many of the ancient marks. The marks had been eroded by weather and time. Sylvia traced them with her finger. She traced the marks that she and the girl had made. She traced the curve that linked spiral to spiral and to all the other spirals and that turned all things to one.

She smiled.

There on the grass by the rock was the hammer stone. It was half-buried in the grass. Moss grew on it. She lifted it and peeled away some of the moss on it. She saw the marks on it, where it had been used many times to strike stone tools. Now she laid it on the grass and next to it she placed the knife, the scraper, the hollow bone.

And looked at them and was content.

'I am Sylvia Carr,' she whispered to the air.

She smiled at the delight of being Sylvia Carr.

And time moved on, and the light strengthened all around her.

'Sylvia! Sylvia Carr!'

The voice, high-pitched, still far away.

'Sylviaaaa!'

She imagined him, moving through the trees, passing from shadow to light, from shadow to light, little shifting body in this huge and ancient place.

'I'm here,' she said softly. 'Keep looking. You'll soon find me.'

'Sylviaaaa!'

Yes, she was Sylvia, but she was also the girl in a seashell necklace, the girl who had guided her into the forest, the girl who had knelt at her side in the moonlight to create spirals in the rock.

How strange, and how wonderful, to be this new version of herself.

'Hello, Sylvia.'

The voice was right at her side now.

She turned her head, and there he was, her young pale-haired friend Colin, sitting calmly on the grass beside the rock.

He said hello again.

She tried to speak but the words couldn't come out properly.

'Colin,' she said at last. 'How long you been there?'

He laughed.

'Oh, for ages,' he said. 'Are you coming back now?'

'I knocked at your door. I threw pebbles at your window.'

'Pebbles?' she said.

'Yes. Little stones.'

They were heading back down through the forest. She was still half in a dream.

'I came to collect you for breakfast,' he said.

'Breakfast?'

He laughed.

'Yes, Sylvia. Breakfast.'

Her body moved slowly. She stumbled. She put her feet forward carefully, deliberately. She felt like a child learning to walk again.

She licked her lips, rolled her tongue.

'Just went for a w-walk,' she said.

It was like learning to speak again.

It was like learning to live again.

Out of the forest, across the rushing stream, past the fallen totem poles, the dangling Christ.

'Here she is!' said Colin.

Anthony and Gabriel, outside their house. Shafts of early sunlight falling on them.

'You were up with the larks?' said Anthony.

She frowned. Larks?

'W-went for a wander,' she said softly.

'Come on, then. Come inside.'

Gabriel took her elbow and led her to the kitchen table.

There was cereal and fruit there. Anthony made tea and coffee.

'She wasn't far away,' said Colin.

He laughed.

'I brought the lost one home again!'

Sylvia ate hungrily, greedily, as if she'd returned from some great journey, some great exertion.

Anthony made toast and she ate slice after slice of it.

She drank mug after mug of sweet tea.

Her voice loosened.

Her mind cleared.

'Think I fell asleep,' she said. 'It was really comfortable.'

A little spider was moving across her jeans. She reached down and let it run across the back of her hand. She saw the grazes on her hands, the tiny nicks and marks on the skin. The muscles of her fingers were sore.

'It was rather beautiful,' she said.

Gabriel watched her.

She swigged more tea.

Part of her remained in the forest, by the rock, with the girl.

Part of her was still in the distant past.

Perhaps it'd always be so.

She swigged a final mug of tea.

She wasn't ready to be with anyone right now.

'I'll head back,' she said.

'Already?' said Anthony.

'Yes. Sorry.'

'I'll come with you?' said Gabriel. 'Shall I?'

He walked with her on the narrow roadway towards her house.

'I was out all night,' she told him.

'Ah. I had this weird feeling.'

'Did you?'

'Last night, before I slept. That you'd disappeared. That you'd gone.'

'Gone where?'

'Dunno. To Newcastle, maybe.'

'From here? In the night?'

He laughed.

'I even had this sense,' he said, 'that you'd never

been here at all, that you were some kind of figment.'

'And here I am, real as ever.'

She touched herself, her arms, hands, cheeks.

'See? Touch me and you'll see.'

He touched his index finger to her shoulder.

'Large as life,' he said.

'Yes, large as life.'

The village was stirring. A car drove past them and mounted the road leading over the fell.

'Did you cross into the spirit world?' he said.

She took the heavy stone from her pocket.

'I found this,' she said. 'Nothing very spiritual about this.'

She stroked away some more of the moss on it.

'There was a girl,' she said.

'Ah. Again, there was a girl. And was her name Sylvia Carr?'

'Yes. No.'

'Ah, that mysterious answer. Yes no. No yes.'

She smiled.

'I will tell you,' she said quietly. 'But not now, Gabriel.'

'Are you OK?'

'I think I might have died,' she found herself saying.

She laughed at herself.

'What nonsense!' she said. 'Of course I can't have died. Can I?'

'No,' he said. 'I don't know, Sylvia.'

'What does it *mean* to die?' she said.

'I don't know,' he said again.

He laughed. She laughed with him.

'Who knows *anything* about *anything*, Gabriel?'

'Not me.'

'Not me.'

They saw Andreas come out of his front door with a tray of tea in his hands. He put it on to his table, sat on his chair.

He waved at them.

They all wished each other good morning.

Sylvia and Gabriel went to his little gate.

Sylvia held out the stone to him.

'I found this, Andreas. In the forest.'

He took it from her in his trembling hands and inspected it.

'You need keen eyes to see such things,' he said.

He ran his fingers across it.

'See the little marks on it?' he said. 'It is a hammer stone.'

'It was the stone that drove the blade through the

rock,' he said.

He passed it back to her.

'The past is all around us,' she said, echoing his words from just a few days past.

She felt the weight of the stone in her hand, the coldness of it against her skin. She felt the presence of the girl beside her, within her. She felt the girl's hand in her own.

'It is deep within us,' she said. 'It lies waiting to be found.'

She knew that one day she'd try to tell Andreas about the hollow bone, about the girl, about the rock. And she knew she'd have to tell him soon, for Andreas was ninety-five years old.

His eyes shone.

'And now, in this present moment,' he said, 'it is a splendid morning, my fine young friends.'

'It is,' said Gabriel.

'Think how awful it would be,' said Andreas, 'to live within such splendidness and not to see such splendidness.'

Sylvia breathed deeply and spread her arms wide to the morning sky.

'Yes!' she said. 'How awful it would be!'

Andreas picked up his tea.

'I will drink my tea,' he said. 'And you, my fine young friends, may walk on through the splendidness.'

She and Gabriel walked on.

They came to Sylvia's door.

'I had this idea,' he said. 'I thought we should play the hollow bones together, at the club, on music night.'

'Could we? Could I?'

They stood so close to each other.

They could feel each other's breath.

'When you've made a hollow bone,' said Gabriel, 'you have to play it for the world. We'll rehearse first, yes?'

'Yes, Gabriel. OK. We will.'

She stepped back from him.

'I have to go in,' she said.

She didn't move.

Then she leaned forward quickly, put her arm around his waist, and kissed his cheek.

He blushed and she smiled.

'I did cross over,' she whispered.

She said no more, she went inside.

She sat alone on a chair in the shadowed room.

She felt the blood running through her veins, felt the breath sighing in her chest. She was young. She was free. She was Sylvia.

She slept for many hours. She did not dream.

Out on the fell there was a signal. She had words with her mum. It was as well that she had stayed. The boy was OK for now, but he had not been. He'd run away. He'd been found sleeping in a cave on the beach at Cullercoats. He said that she was the only one that he could talk to. He had wanted to do away with himself, he said. He had wanted to drown himself, but the water was too cold. He had wanted to jump from the cliffs, but the cliffs were too low. He said he was pathetic. Not even clever enough to kill himself. That was because he hadn't wanted to, not really. He wanted what all of us wanted but many of us find it difficult to find. He wanted love. He wanted to live.

'You'd like him, I think,' said her mum. 'He isn't easy, but then he hasn't had it easy. Maybe you could go to see him, once you're back again.'

Sylvia smiled, thought of all the other of her

mother's troubled children she'd encountered through the years.

'Yes, Mum. Maybe I could.'

So odd, to think of going back to the ordinary world again.

'He's almost as old as you,' said her mum, 'but he's very young. He has a lot of growing up to do.'

'And Dad?' said Sylvia.

'Still in Rome, it seems.' She laughed bitterly. 'I'm giving up, Sylvia. I don't care.'

'Of course you do.'

'Do I? Do I really?'

The signal came and went. Mum seemed to say she'd be returning soon.

Yes, Sylvia told her. She was fine. Yes, Gabriel and her family were looking after her. Yes, she was happy. No, she didn't feel abandoned.

The signal went. Her mum went.

She looked across the fells towards the city.

She'd go back very soon.

There were mice in the corner of the room. Two of them, very still, in the shadows against the skirting board. And three spiders dangled on threads from the ceiling. And a jackdaw sat on the fence just beyond the window. And another.

She didn't mention them.

She breathed into the fragile hollow bone. She moved her fingers on the fingerholes. The sounds that came were so light and delicate. She breathed harder and the sounds intensified.

'But how will they hear us in that great big club room?' she said.

'We'll tell Mike to tell them to be quiet,' said Gabriel. 'He'll keep them in order.'

They were in her house, the living room. Her mum had not yet returned.

They rehearsed together.

They tried to play folk tunes – Bonnie at Morn, Waters of Tyne – but their flutes weren't made for this. There weren't enough notes, the notes weren't spaced properly. So they just breathed, and varied their breathing, and moved their tongues and cheeks and fingers and lungs, and the tunes they made were new and different every time. Sometimes the tunes came together in harmony, then they diverged. Sometimes the notes were uneven, jerky, even ugly, then the sound broke through into moments of beauty and grace.

Gabriel laughed.

'I don't even know why we're rehearsing,' he said. 'It's hardly like we're going to perfect a tune, or come up with a set list.'

But they just kept on playing, and sometimes they lost themselves in the playing. Sylvia knew that she withheld something in her playing. She was wary of being carried through time again, or crossing some weird border again. She'd done that in the forest, didn't want to do it in the old little forestry house. And she liked the sense of being present, in this place, in this time, with this boy.

She grinned. She nodded at the mice, at the spiders.

'You've seen our audience?' she whispered.

'I have,' he whispered back.

She knew that the music drew them nearer to each other: the harmony of their breath, of their bodies swaying together so close. Sometimes their shoulders touched. They smiled into each other's eyes. They looked unsmiling into each other's eyes, into the depths created and uncovered by the music. But she held herself back from him, as well.

So much was going on, so many changes in herself.

As the light faded outside, she put her hollow bone aside.

The mice disappeared. The spiders climbed their threads again. The jackdaws went.

'We'll be fine,' she said.

'Yes, we will.'

'I'll be shy,' she said.

'Me too. But we'll be fine.'

'We will.'

He gazed at her.

'I guess we've done enough,' she said.

He shrugged.

'OK.'

She led him to the door.

They kissed each other's cheek.

He went away.

The girl did not come back. Her mum did not come back. Sylvia was on her own. She played the hollow bone for herself, in the kitchen, the little living room, the little bedroom. She stood tall and played it. She lay on the floor and played it. Sometimes she felt that she rose from the floor, that she began to float and fly, that she was turning into the buzzard from whose bone the instrument had been made.

When she slept, she dreamed that forests grew inside her and upon her, that forests grew across the whole world. She dreamed that the living and the dead and the still-to-be-born danced together in forest clearings.

One night her bedroom became a forest clearing. She lay in it, like a fallen buzzard. People came from among the trees carrying stone knives. They crouched and knelt at her side. They sawed and cut her and separated her and spread her bones out on the turf. They took her ulna and cleared the marrow from it. They carved a mouthpiece and fingerholes. And now the girl did come. It was she who lifted the hollow bone formed from Sylvia's ulna and blew through it. The music she made was very beautiful and folk danced in spirals to the music that came from Sylvia's bone.

And the girl became the animal from which the hollow bone had been made. That animal was Sylvia Carr. The girl became Sylvia Carr. Her bones were Sylvia's bones. Her flesh was Sylvia's flesh. And Sylvia Carr herself was content, to be held in the hands of this girl, to be breathed through by this girl, to be this girl.

She was Sylvia, Sylvia was she.

And when Sylvia woke, she knew that everything was changing and would continue to change for ever more.

And she got up from her sleep and knew a happiness she'd never known before.

In a sketchbook, Sylvia drew the girl, her hair, her seashell necklace. The girl stood by the patterned rock, and she gazed out with calm bright eyes. She held a stone knife in one hand, a hammer stone in the other. Sylvia sighed. It was far from perfect. But it was the best she could do. She rolled it up and went to Andreas.

It was a cold morning. There was drizzle in the air. She tapped at his door. He came slowly. He was supporting himself with a stick and his hands were trembling.

He smiled.

'It's just the cold,' he told her. 'Some days are difficult. Come inside, Sylvia.'

She sat in an armchair. He insisted on making her tea.

'I made this for you,' she said.

She unrolled the picture. Seeing it again, she liked it more, the bright grass beside the dark rock, the patterns there, the girl herself, who seemed more real and more alive, now that she was seen by another.

She was more like she had really been.

'It's wonderful,' said Andreas.

He looked closely at the picture, then closely at her.

'It's you, Sylvia?'

How could she really explain?

'I guess so, Andreas. Or me as I was five thousand years ago.'

'So it *is* you. Thank you.'

The room was lined with books. There were stone tools on shelves. There was an old cardboard box on the floor at his feet.

'You catch me as I search my own past, Sylvia,' he said.

He took a deep breath.

'I thought that I should do it alone. But perhaps it is right that you come here now, just as I am doing this. You're at the very beginning. I am close to the end.' He indicated the box. 'Help me, Sylvia.'

She lifted the box from the floor.

He lifted the lid.

There were papers and photographs inside.

'This is me,' he said. 'As I was, five thousand years ago. Or eighty years ago.'

He lifted out a photograph. He held it face down in his hand.

'Maybe you'll hate me,' he said.

He stared into a distance, composing himself.

'I have thought many times of destroying these things,' he said. 'But there's no escape from them. The past needs to be known.'

He turned over the photograph. A faded colour photograph of an unsmiling boy. He wore shorts, boots, a beige shirt, a tie, a cap.

'I was fifteen years old,' said Andreas. 'The same as you.'

After the first shock, she looked closely. Yes, it was Andreas. The face of the boy was still apparent in the face of the old man.

He took out another photograph. A troupe of boys just like himself, carrying rucksacks, marching together in their uniforms along a forest path.

He pointed.

'Me again,' he said. 'See how happy I am?'

She nodded again.

'The Hitler Youth,' he said.

He repeated the words. He paused. She said nothing.

'You have not walked away, Sylvia,' he said.

She shook her head. She couldn't speak.

'All of us were in it. All we children. We were happy. I hear our tramping feet. I hear the songs we sang. We loved marching, singing, camping, attending rallies. We were together. We felt free.'

He paused. His hands trembled.

'We loved *him*,' he said.

Another photograph. This time there were hundreds of boys, stern-faced. They stood in ranks inside a stadium. Walking before them was Hitler, giving his salute.

'Yes,' said Andreas. 'We loved *him*.'

He pointed to a boy in the front row.

'Look how pleased I am, Sylvia. Look at the delight that's shining from my eyes.'

She could not speak. She looked at the boy, Andreas, at the man, Andreas.

'And soon enough,' he said, 'I would be marching with that delight into a war. And had I come across one like you, I would have tried to destroy you.'

He put back the lid. He held the three photographs in his hand.

'Do you hate me now?' he asked.

Her mind reeled. How to make sense of such a thing? How could this boy also be this kind old man?

'That's not you,' she said. 'Not as you are now.'

'But it is. That boy, Andreas, survives within this Andreas. The young and cruel man that he became survives within.'

'You changed.'

'Yes. I was transformed, as the world was transformed. I was saved by being captured, by being imprisoned, by coming to Northumberland. I was saved by forests and music and skylarks and stone axes. I am continually being saved.'

He leaned a little closer to her.

'I am being saved, Sylvia, by you.'

He drank some tea.

'It is a long, long tale,' he said. 'And I am getting to the end of it, but yes, at the end maybe it is a tale of hope. The deluded boy and this trembling man become a sign of hope.'

'They do, Andreas.'

'Beware the adult,' he said softly, 'who wants to regiment the child.'

They drank tea together.

Outside, the drizzle ended and the sun began shining through.

He held out the photographs to her.

'I should like you to take them if you would,' he said.

She took them, these strange paradoxical gifts from this strange paradoxical man.

'Destroy them if you wish,' he said.

She had no idea what she might do with them, but she felt they'd be with her all her life.

She put them into the pocket of her waterproof.

'Thank you for your beautiful drawing,' he said. 'I'll keep it always.'

They shook each other's hand and she left his house.

The sun was shining bright.

Light spilled from the hall into the dark street.

Sylvia and Gabriel walked in together. They were with Anthony and Colin. Sylvia's mum hadn't returned. They sat at a table with Andreas. He had a glass of pale beer which he raised in welcome as they appeared.

The tall man, Mike, stood on the stage, fiddling with the microphone.

There were musicians all around, sitting at tables, standing against the walls, drinking at the bar. Little quiet sessions were already taking place. Violinists with accordionists, tin whistlers with drummers. Many folk sang in restrained and lovely voices. An old man stood in a shadowed corner squeezing the bellows of his pipes, raising notes of lamentation. Young children played and whirled in the empty spaces.

Oliver and Daphne Dodd came to sit with them. He was in his old tweeds, she in her shiny red-and-brown floral dress.

Oliver laughed.

'This is getting to be a habit,' he said.

'You're getting used to the place?' said Daphne to Sylvia. 'Getting used to us all?'

Sylvia said yes. She found herself saying that she'd never known anywhere like this place.

'Nor have we,' said Daphne. 'Mind you, it's not as if we've known any other. Not like you young ones, travelling the world.'

Young people came to Gabriel, asked if he would play with them tonight. He said maybe he would,

later. He said he might play with Sylvia tonight.
They smiled. She blushed. They smiled again. She
blushed again.

'What will you play?' said Oliver Dodds.

Sylvia shyly took it from her pocket. She placed it
on the table.

'Oh, my goodness,' said Daphne. 'A hollow bone!'
She reached across.

'May I?'

Daphne took it in her hands, as the girl in the night
had taken it in her hands.

'It's from a buzzard,' said Sylvia.

'I made it with the tools you gave me,' she said
to Andreas.

'My father had one,' said Daphne. 'Long, long
ago. I was very small. Oh, when he played, the
delight of it, the magic of it. We lost ourselves in
dancing to it.'

She raised it to her lips and played a note and smiled
with a kind of bliss.

She held it in her spread hands, giving it back
to Sylvia.

'He said it would come down to me, but oh where's
that hollow bone now?'

She laughed.

'It's why I play the piccolo. The nearest kind of instrument to it.'

She played a few notes on her piccolo.

'Lovely, of course. But not the same. Not the magic, Sylvia.'

Now Gabriel took out his hollow bone.

Daphne gasped again.

She took it in her hands.

She played a few notes.

Tears came to her eyes.

'I found it,' said Gabriel. 'In an abandoned farmhouse. On a far fell.'

She closed her hand around it.

'Could it be?' she said. 'Of course it couldn't. Could it?'

She played again.

She closed her eyes and smiled.

'I'm a child again, Oliver,' she said to her husband.

'My love,' he said. 'There'll always be a child in you.'

'He said he did not know what kind of beast it came from,' she said. 'Sometimes he said it was the bone of a skinny fox, sometimes a wild cat, sometimes a golden eagle. Who knows what might be true?'

She held it to her face, as if to breathe in the breath of her father, to breathe in all the breath that had ever played through it.

'Sometimes, at night,' she said, 'I've thought that I can hear it. The sound of it drifting across the fells. Like in a dream.'

'Could it be?' she asked again. 'He said he couldn't remember how it had come into his possession. Though he said possession was the wrong word. It would be held in his hands for a time, then it would be held in the hands of another, and so on till the thing broke up, or till the end of time.'

She closed her eyes. She smiled, hearing the music of her childhood.

'It was long ago,' she said.

She passed it back to Gabriel.

'Play well, son,' she said.

The first musicians moved on to the stage. A group of children, nine or ten years old, played fiddles together. They sawed and squeaked and sometimes came together in harmony and tune. There was much applause for them. Then singers, the two girls from last week. They sang about two lovers separated by water, and about a pair of crows that ate the body of a slaughtered knight. Then clog dancers and an accordionist, and couples dancing arm-in-arm on the floor. And Mike chanted a border ballad filled with violence and war. Then Daphne played her piccolo and there were calls from his friends for Gabriel to join them in a tune, until at last Gabriel got up and asked Sylvia to do the same and they moved together through the tables to the stage space. Gabriel whispered words to Mike, who raised his hands high and called for the room to hush for we had a new musician among us who wished to play and we must give her some quiet. And Sylvia felt shy, shy, but she also felt bold, and she stood with Gabriel at her side, and she found herself softly saying, 'I will play the hollow bone for you.'

And there was some gentle applause, some gentle cheers, some calls for her to speak up, and then an almost-silence.

And as she stood there, she saw how frail this instrument was, how small, how light. Many in the room would hardly be able to see it at all. And she raised it to her lips, the sound it made was so soft, so breathy. In this room it seemed hardly there at all. But Gabriel moved the microphone closer to her, and the sound was magnified and began to flow into the room.

She had no tune to play, just notes carried from her body on her breath and squeezed out through her own created hollow bone. She relaxed. She ran her fingers across the fingerholes. She varied the intensity of her breath. She closed her eyes and swayed gently as she played. She opened them again and saw people moving closer to her. She saw those at the tables resting their heads on their hands and watching her in surprise and then with a kind of wonder. She tapped her feet upon the stage. Folk began to move, to sway, to shift gently across the floor. She breathed harder, harder and the notes rose and strengthened. So strong, so strange, like the voice of some unnamed creature, the voice of water or of the wind. She leaned into the sounds she made. They spiralled around the room, came back to her, were played again, again. And Sylvia felt herself changing yet again, as she had kept changing ever since she'd come to this place. She stood there, a frail fifteen-year old girl on this small stage with a frail instrument at her lips and felt that she might rise from the floor here, like a buzzard, a skylark, an angel, while all the world and all of time sang through her, through the hollow bone named Sylvia Carr.

And her friend Gabriel joined her and played his own notes.

And now the others came, with their pipes and whistles and fiddles and drums and their guitars and accordions and their clogs and their singing voices and they played together there in the ancient club in a forestry village in far Northumberland. And the dancers danced around them, the old and the frail and the jolly and the young. And the moves they made fell into the pattern of spirals. They swirled together around the room, linked each to each, everyone to everyone, making the spiralling, endlessly regenerating dance of life and time.

Afterwards, Sylvia and Gabriel went outside. They sat close together on a bench between the darkness and the light. Sylvia said that she must go back soon, to Newcastle, her city, to her friends.

'There's another day of protest,' she said. 'I kind of promised Maxine I'd be there.'

'That's good.'

'Can't be hanging round in forests all my life. And anyway, another term's starting. GCSEs. Rites of passage. What total joy!'

'Is it joy?'

She laughed. She thought.

'It kind of is, Gabriel. I know there's lots that's wrong, but we're all together there. Me, Maxine, Francesca, Mickey, all the rest. We haven't been too damaged by it all. And our life outside of school is bigger than the life inside.'

She breathed the night air, loved the night air.

'We love each other. That's what makes it right. That's what gives us hope.'

She nudged him.

'And then it's sixth form.'

'Hell's teeth. Sixth form! Do they wear suits?'

'Nope. They wear anything they want.'

She nudged him again.

'Maybe you should bring that big brain of yours along and join us, Gabriel?'

'As if.'

'Yes. As if! You could come and meet everyone, be part of it all.'

He looked away.

'We'd look after you,' she softly said.

'We all need to be together,' she softly said.

She thought about that. She knew that she was right.

'Yes, Gabriel,' she said. 'Come to join us. Be part of us.'

Folk were leaving the club. Several said good night. Andreas said how magical their music had been. He tottered back along the street.

Oliver and Daphne Dodd came out.

'I'm glad you have it, son,' said Daphne to Gabriel.

'You think it *is* the same one?' he answered.

'Close enough,' she said. 'Maybe there's only a handful of hollow bones that get passed from hand to hand and that make their way through time.'

They said good night.

'Use it well,' said Daphne as she and her husband stepped out of the light.

'What *did* happen,' said Gabriel, 'the other night?'

She took a deep breath. She didn't know where to start, but she softly told him, and she started with the words, 'There was a girl.'

'And her name was Sylvia Carr?'

'Yes no. No yes. I was her and she was me.'

He said nothing, he waited.

'And I spent a night in the forest with her. Or I spent an age in the forest with her. And we created art on the rock together. And I think I died.'

He let her go on.

'I was rewilded, Gabriel. I died and I was brought back to life. The forest grew on me. And now I'm here and now, and talking about going back to school. That feels like the weirdest thing of all.'

Mike came out from the club.

'Well done, you two,' he said.

He closed the doors. The light was shut off.

'Strangest gig I've ever heard,' he said. 'Good night to you both.'

He left them alone together in the darkness.

Above them, endless spirals of galaxies and stars.

Within them, endless spirals of longing and delight.

'You're beautiful,' said Gabriel.

'You're beautiful,' said Sylvia.

There was nothing else to say.

They kissed each other.

They kissed again.

Mum stayed away. She said she had to stay to help look after the boy. They spoke on the phone at Anthony's house.

'Are you OK, my darling?'

'I am,' said Sylvia.

'And Gabriel? And the others?'

'They're fine.'

Her mum cleared her throat, began to talk about Sylvia's father. He was still in Rome, still with pasta and starlings, still drawn to destruction and war. They had been talking on the phone.

'So strange,' said her mother. 'Where I am is where we once all were. It was the heart of everything. Now there's just me, here alone. You're in the forest, he's far away and wanting to go further.'

'I'll soon be back,' said Sylvia.

'I'll come to get you.'

'There's a gathering at the Monument on Saturday,' said Sylvia. 'I want to be there.'

'I'll be back for you before then.'

'So are you leaving him?' said Sylvia.

There was a long silence.

'I'm sorry,' Mum whispered.

Tears came to Sylvia's eyes. 'Life moves on,' she

murmured. 'Things change.'

'That sounds like the kind of thing I should be saying to you.'

'I love you, Mum,' said Sylvia.

'I love you, love.'

Sylvia walked with Gabriel. She sat on the swings with him. They went into the forest together and found clearings with soft turf into which the sun could shine.

She showed him the marks that she'd made on the rock.

'Maybe that's what I was doing to my skin,' he said. 'Making an ancient mark on my new young form.'

'Flesh isn't rock, though, Gabriel. The body's tender. We have to cherish it and protect it.'

She touched his cheek.

'The flesh is sacred,' she said.

A day and another day slipped by.

She told him about her friends and about the city.

'I used to hide away,' he told her. 'I used to study alone in my room.'

'Recluse?' she said.

'Maybe. I told myself that that was the way I liked to be. Just me, my books, my brain.'

He shrugged.

'And my pain,' he said.

'And is that the way you'd like to be again?'

He shook his head.

He taught her the names of birds and plants.

He named the fells and the streams.

He told her the names of the battles that had been fought here.

They waved their fists at low-flying jets.

They cursed the thuds that came from the Danger Area.

One day they walked and kept walking, all the way to the edge of the lake. They talked about the lost village beneath. They said that though much had been destroyed, the lake and its surroundings were beautiful. They talked about destruction and creation.

'Things die,' said Sylvia. 'Things come to life.'

She shook her head. She cried a little.

The words were so simple, so obvious, but they felt so profound.

Night-time was falling as they headed back. The sky was filled with stars. On the fells, farmhouses shone like distant galaxies. Newcastle glowed on the southern horizon.

Sylvia pointed to it.

'Isn't it lovely?' she said. 'It's a beautiful city, Gabriel.'

'As beautiful as here? As beautiful as the forest and the fells and the lake and the stars?'

'We need it all. The city and the wilderness, the darkness and the light. We need everything.'

'Maybe I will come,' he said. 'Bring my big brain and be with you all.'

'Do that, Gabriel. We need everybody.'

Saturday morning, Sylvia waited. Tidied the house, packed their clothes. Took down photos from walls. Put away her mum's art things. Packed her scraper, knife, hammer stone, hollow bone. Packed the photographs of Andreas as a boy. Made some tea and toast and waited.

Her mum came back all in a rush.

'So much for having a break from it all!' she said. 'I was up at dawn and now we have to hurry back again.'

She gathered the few drawings she'd made, of Sylvia, Andreas, Anthony, Gabriel and Colin. Drawings of the fells, of a fox, a distant deer.

'I've hardly been here!' she said.

'Thanks for bringing me, Mum,' said Sylvia.

'Ha! You were the one who didn't want to come at all.'

'Well, what did I know?'

'And what do you know now?'

Sylvia laughed.

She showed her mum the hollow bone.

'I know how to make one of these,' she said.

'Funny little thing.'

'No time to explain now. I'll tell you when we're heading back.'

They packed the car, closed up the house, walked through the village to say their goodbyes.

Anthony was on a ladder at the side of the church with a hammer in his hand.

'Give me a sec,' he said. 'It's bothered me ever since we arrived.'

He stretched up and held Christ against the cross again.

He nailed him there. He tugged to make sure he wouldn't fall.

'There we are,' he said. 'He's not going anywhere.'

He climbed down to them. Gabriel and Colin came out of the house.

Sylvia and Gabriel walked away a few yards together.

They kissed.

'I will come,' said Gabriel.

They both blushed as they returned to the others.

Anthony and her mum were talking of how the families would soon meet up again.

They all hugged and said goodbye.

Sylvia and her mum walked back to the car.

They knocked at Andreas's door.

They said goodbye. He took Sylvia's hand.

'Thank you for listening,' he said.

'Thank you for not hating me,' he said.

'We'll see you again,' said Mum.

'Perhaps,' said Andreas, and he smiled.

They got into the car. They drove away from the club, the totem poles, the nailed-again Christ. They drove past the swings, the footpath sign with the cartoon striding man. Away from the forest, the darkness, the silence. Away from the rock art and music. Away from the foxes and deer and buzzards.

Away from the past. Sylvia left it all behind, but she took it all with her.

It was in her, of her.

The car was quick. It took them across the fell and towards the next valley.

They paused at the top to look back. They wound down the windows. There were birds of prey high above. There were skylarks, curlews, there was wind in the grass.

The land went on forever. The sky went on forever.

And two deer came, all of a sudden. They leapt across the road in front of the car. Their stretched bodies were outlined against the sky. They landed, then dashed on across the heather and the turf, then stopped and looked back towards Sylvia and her mum.

Goodbye.

Onward.

They drove, over the fell, into the next valley.

Soon the sea was visible, dark on the horizon. The shapes of ships were on it. Wind turbines were turning there. Jagged Dunstanburgh Castle stood on its rock.

They left the fells behind, and drove over the ancient closed-up coalfields.

'Shall we have some music?' said Mum.

'Yes!' said Sylvia.

She showed her the hollow bone. She lifted it to her lips and played a note, another note.

'That's so strange, love,' said her mum.

'I made it, with Gabriel, from the bone of a bird.'

'From a *what*?'

Sylvia played. Played it low and sweet. But audible above the sound of the engine. Her mum sighed and said that it was beautiful, much nicer than that old recorder.

Sylvia paused. It wouldn't do for her mum to lose herself.

'You OK?' she said.

'Aye. Of course. Play on, love.'

'But keep your mind on the road, Mum.'

'I will.'

Sylvia played on, carrying the darkness of the forest towards the city's heart.

Past Wark, Simonburn, Chollerford, Wall. On to the A69 dual carriageway, traffic speeding towards the city. There were trucks and cars and caravans. A police car with its siren blaring, lights flashing. The roofs and spires of the city appeared in the east.

'Back to civilisation,' said Mum. 'Don't stop. It's lovely.'

The traffic slowing, backing up before the final roundabout. Direction signs, traffic lights, markings on the roadway.

Over they went. Up the west road, past shops and

pubs and curry houses, past churches and temples and mosques. Stop and start, accelerate and slow. Still Sylvia played. Still her mum smiled.

There were now young people in pairs and little groups, some of them carrying banners and homemade posters.

VOTES FOR 16 YEAR OLDS
WE ARE THE FUTURE
THERE IS NO PLANET B
REBEL FOR LIFE

They wore wild clothes. They were swinging, singing, silly, serious.

'That's us, Mum,' said Sylvia.

Back through the streets to their neat terraced house.

Sylvia took off her boots and waterproof. She put on her canvas shoes, her jeans, a cowboy shirt. She snatched a sandwich.

'Maxine, I've made it,' she said into her phone as she hurried away from home.

'Wonderful! Back in the real world! Meet at the Haymarket!'

She ran from home to the metro. It was so so packed.

Lots of kids on it. Some of them she knew. They waved and grinned.

So strange, to be among so many after being with so few. So much noise after so much silence. So much speed. It really was like she'd been away five thousand years.

The metro slid to a halt. She slipped through the door. Up the escalator she went.

And they're all there. Maxine, Mickey, Francesca, all the rest.

'Welcome back to the present!' declares Maxine. 'You've been away forever, lass!'

She kisses her on the lips.

The joy of it. The physicality of it. The togetherness of it. The craziness of it.

On they all hurry towards the Monument. So many young people, so many banners. Such a crowd around the Monument itself, the great tower that has jutted for over a century high into the clear Newcastle sky. There's a stage before it. A band of teenagers are setting up their instruments. There are poets and musicians and politicians. A girl who must be no more than ten years old speaks into a microphone to say that the time of youth has come.

More crowds gather. There are families with toddlers and babies. Old women and old men. Sylvia and her friends tremble and laugh with excitement. Mickey has a drum under his arm that he slaps with his open hand.

The band plays.

They dance and sing along.

The crowd sways.

More children speak, more teenagers.

Adults cheer and applaud.

The band comes to the end of a song. Sylvia finds herself moving through the bodies to the stage. She steps up into it. She stands before the microphone.

'I'd like to play for you,' she says.

'Speak up!'

'I'd like to play for you.'

How did she do such a thing? She didn't know that she'd do it until she found herself doing it. All these people in the heart of the city, all these voices, all these faces, and Maxine, grinning, her face in the crowd, the faces of her other friends, astonished, urging her on.

Small shy Sylvia, Sylvia Carr.

And just this frail thing in her hand.

Anyway, she just gives herself up to what she seems to be doing. She lifts the thing to her lips and leans towards the microphone and she plays it. And to hear it, the crowd around her must grow silent, as they do. And the silence moves out towards the fringes of the crowd as Sylvia plays. Music from the bone of a bird and a northern forest and a small girl's throat moves through the city's heart.

And Sylvia loses herself as she has before.

She leaves her body. She rises like a bird and looks down and sees Sylvia playing, she sees the crowd around her. She sees the spirals they make, the spirals of galaxies, of time, of the rock, of the soul.

And she descends again, singing like a skylark sings as it falls, spiralling as a buzzard does as it comes to earth again.

She comes to rest on the stage with the hollow bone at her lips.

And she goes on playing, playing.

And there she is, the girl, there in the Newcastle crowd. The same face, same eyes, same hair, same seashell necklace, same seashell earrings. She's wearing a white T-shirt with two linked spirals printed on it.

And Sylvia lowers the hollow bone from her lips.

'I am you and you are me,' she says.

The girl smiles. The crowd is silent.

'We are ancient and brand new,' she says.

'We are the forest and we are the city,' she says.

'We are shy and we are wild,' she says.

'We will be with each other always,' she says.

She plays the frail instrument again, plays the eternal, ever-changing tunes again.

'We are frail and we are small,' she says. 'But we are beautiful and strong, and we can change the world.'